I0666367

Skin boi

First Edition

ty dehner

Skin boi

First Edition

Published by The Nazca Plains Corporation
Las Vegas, Nevada
2007

ISBN: 978-1-934625-26-2

Published by

The Nazca Plains Corporation ®
4640 Paradise Rd, Suite 141
Las Vegas NV 89109-8000

PUBLISHER'S NOTE
Skin boi is a work of fiction created wholly by *ty dehner's* imagination. All characters are fictional and any resemblance to any
persons living or deceased is purely by accident. No portion of
this book reflects any real person or events.

Photographer, Eliot Lovell (www.eliotlovell.net)
Cover Model, Elliot London (www.worldskins.com/muscleskinuk)
Art Director, Blake Stephens

Acknowledgements

Sitting here before my computer in my enclosed cell, locked in my hood, feeling the boots on my feet and hearing the leather as I move, I think upon those that have helped me reach this point of seeing my words in print.

First, I kneel before the boots of Alex Ironrod, who encouraged me to publish my work. When I read his first story, I was hooked and found it to be some of the best I had ever read! OK, yes, it got my dick hard also! I was proud to be the first to present his work to the public and later to be asked to be part of his first book! Appropriately, he is now the Master and I am the learner. As I taste the leather of his boots I thank Alex so much for his guidance!

Much of what I have written could have only come because of three Masters from my past that influenced my life. For what ever reason, I was not to become their permanent slave. But when I was bound by these three men I realized that serving and worshipping them was not just about sex and bondage, it was also about love and affection. They each trained me in their own way with intensity and taking me beyond limits that I thought I never could achicve.

After reading about the thrilling bondage adventures in magazines like Bound and Gagged, I never thought I would experience even half that much! Thanks to the many great men I explored with in the Pacific Northwest, I did what I had only dreamed about and more. These guys helped me to become the submissive I am today. I was allowed to find my true self. They introduced me to others in the community. A community I am proud to be a apart of.

Then there was Ropedweb. During the 6 years that I was publisher and creator I loved hearing from the readers about how they enjoyed the stories. It always made the suffering in full leather, or locked in a hood for hours, writing until the issue was completed worth it. It was hard work, but someone had to do it. In the end the reward was when someone said they had found someone to explore their fetish or bondage with and had a great time.

It is not often you will meet someone at the other end of the phone line when you are tied up and gagged and listen to him gagged at the other end. Such was my first meeting of N.C. Bound. I want to thank him for encouraging me to write in the kinky world.

Finally, there is my current Linebacker. As I kneel at his cleats, he stands above me in his full pads and uniform, allowing me to serve him with all my heart. Everyday I thank God that I have him in my life.

I hope that I have not forgotten any of the great men that have let me explore and live. I know my ass will be red when I run into them sometime in the future!

Dedication

To Packer Cop, no border will ever hold back my love and devotion for you.

Skin boi

ty dehner

Contents

Skin boi

When we started talking via the IRC a couple of months ago, it was because i was really interest in how a Man can say that he is gay and also be a Nazi. Based on what i had been taught, those two could not exist in a person. For wouldn't he hate himself for what he is. But as i talked with Dex, i learned that it was not the racist preaching that he was embracing, it was the order in his life that it brought. How everything done in his world was for the good of himself and His Family. And that is what struck me as being very different about him. It was three months before we exchanged pictures of each other. As our discussions progressed, i found myself wanting to serve this Man and His ideal. Perhaps it was because it was so wrong, but the more i talked and thought the more i wanted to be with Him. My friends thought that i was nuts, and i couldn't convince them that Dex was really a good Man, with very high morals and values. Yes, He enjoyed being rough with a boi, leather and bondage and SM were all strong interests in Him, being a strong part of His life. But i remember my friends thought i was nuts when i began to tell them of how i needed to submit to a Man. They eventually understood how it was something that was always in me, since i was a child. i didn't ask them to live my life, just to accept me for what i am. And that is why i decided that i had to spend a weekend with Dex. i needed to really be with Him to understand Him. i knew that we were becoming special in each others lives. We talked on the phone constantly, sharing idea and thoughts. It was only natural that we meet and try to be together for a weekend.

The Friday morning arrived. Since i was not going to be staying long, i really didn't need much. i carried everything in a backpack. Dex, or Sir as i had begun to call Him, said all would be provided for me. i would need to understand that that is the way of being a Nazi and the order of His Family. He lived alone in Denver, but had been seeking a boi for quite a while. My best friend dropped me off at the airport. He really thought i was nuts for going, but knew that there was no way for him to stop me. i was nervous, as always, when i made these trips. i had traveled a couple times before to meet potential Masters. All became great friends and Men i visit with and play, but we knew we would never be Master/slave to each other. i had a feeling that Dex or Sir would be different.

i arrived in the late morning at the huge Denver airport. Sir was waiting for me at the gate, with a large duffel bag. He looked strong and great. i got a chill up my spine thinking of me serving Him. He was around 6', strong chest, but with a slight belly on Him. His head was, of course, shaved, but He had a goatee. He wore a navy blue polo shirt with white stripe around the collar, suspenders held His snug fitting 501's and there were the great pair of black rangers, almost to His knees, with white laces.

i am a bit over six foot, a husky guy, with a defined chest. i have always keep my hair cut really short, but never had facial hair. Just felt that was not a boi's place to have. i was wearing 501's, a pair of used army boots and a black t-shirt with leather jacket.

As i approached Sir, He smiled, then when i was in His reach, He took a strong grasp around the back of my neck with His hand and pulled me to His lips. His tongue slammed into my throat. i couldn't believe, right here in the airport with others watching He was kissing me. i could feel my dick grow in my jeans, i hoped His was too. i couldn't back off, His grip was strong and He dug His fingers into my neck. i tired to get my tongue into His mouth, but He never let me. Finally, He let go and released the kiss.

"Welcome boi", is all He said. He grabbed me by the neck again and we started down the concourse. We walked briskly, without talking. He kept a firm grip on my neck, guiding me through the crowd. We continued to the very end of the concourse, where it was very quiet, no one was around. He turned me into a restroom and into the handicapped stall.

He locked the stall door, after releasing His grip. "Strip, now boi", was His command.

i did so quickly, though getting out my boots was a bit difficult. i was totally naked in the stall, close to my Master of a Man. He put His hand on my shoulder and forced me to my knees. He undid the buttons on His jeans and i thought i was going to get to suck Him off right then and there. He pulled closer and i opened my mouth as He inserted His dick. His strong hands held my face close to His crotch, as i could take in His strong body scent. i worked my tongue around His cut dick head. Then i felt it, He was pissing in my mouth and i tried to back way. i couldn't, His grip was strong and i was going to take it all in. i was partly choking, trying to swallow as fast i could.

"When a boi serves, He serves totally, without question," he states to me in a firm voice. i slightly nod yes...as His piss continues. "That is the order of being my boi and being a Nazi, boi. That is what this weekend is all about." With that, He finishes. He doesn't release my neck, then i take my tongue and clean up around His piss hole. "Very good boi," that is what He was waiting for.

He releases me. i am instructed to put on what is in the duffel. i open it and do so, putting my plane clothes and boots into the bag in return. When i am done dressing, i am dressed very much like Him, right down to the boots, though mine were a bit shorter. The jeans fit snuggle and i am beginning to feel like a true skinhead boi. Something comes over me and i kneel down and kiss His boots. His hand reaches down, caresses my head and moves under my chin. He tilts my head up towards Him. He looks down at me and smiles, as i look at Him. He opens His mouth and a large wad of spit tumbles down. i take it right in the face. "Let's go."

i am not allowed to wipe the snot, as it slowly slides down my face and neck, drying as parts reach down my shirt. i take the duffel and we head out of the restroom and back down the concourse. He no longer guides me, but i follow a pace behind, as He moves quickly through the terminal.

We arrive at His truck and get in, tossing the duffel in the back under the canopy. He drives us out and we head out across the Colorado plains. As we drive, He opens up to me and i begin to open up to Him. i love the feeling of my new clothes and the boots on my feet, the boot leather feeling snug against my legs. He reaches over and strongly grabs my crotch, laughing at finding me hard. "boi, i will show you a devotion and reward for being a Nazi boi unlike any other Master you have served."

We arrive at His home, which is on several acres of land to the south of Denver. Sir is a Graphic Designer and is looking for a boi to work in His business. i am a Graphic Artist so we feel that we could work together in a home based business that He already owns. i would be able to be His total slave, day in and out and not have to report to a job again.

After getting into the living room, i fall to my knees and once again kiss His boots. He orders me to undress Him. i do so quickly, unlacing His mighty boots. Once He is naked, i see His body as great and strong as i thought. He had one tattoo on His right chest, light body hair covers Him. He has me put His boots back on Him, with white socks, and tightly lace them. Then i am ordered to strip and put my boots back on. As i do so, He disappears into another room.

When He returns, i am naked, in my boots, on my knees waiting for Him. He reaches down and straps a leather collar on me. Not around my neck, but around my cock and balls. It is tight and He says that it will remind me of my service to Him. With that He has me kiss the floor. He spanks my butt and has me raise it to the air. He comes behind me, straddles my legs and works His lubed dick up my ass. He is not gentle with me. Showing me His power over me and how He will guide me to greatness. As He has mention during all our talks, He will sperm with His boi every chance He gets. This fuck is to show me what my life will be like, day in and out. How i will be strong for Him, be there to serve Him.

He slams my ass, with His balls sometimes striking mine. i feel my cock get stronger in its collar. We begin to work as a team, as He works His cock in and out of my tight asshole. i don't have much experience in being used as an asshole. But i want to be the best that i can for Sir. And this is where i want to be in life. I feel His power as He grabs my hips and draws me closer to Him. i moan and sometime give a short scream. He tells me to take it like His fuck boi and to shut up or i will be gagged for the entire weekend. At times i still moan, but i get the feeling He doesn't mind. He likes to see me suffer a bit, He knows that i am truly submitting to Him.

"Remember boi, this is your life. You want to be My fuck boi, to be fucked when ever, where ever My mood deems. You will be ready for Me, you will crave Me and worship Me and the dick that I slam into you now. And I will sperm you to give you the power to continue to live your devoted life. You serve a high order now boi, Me and the Nazi power. Nothing in life will give you greater pleasure, you will want for nothing. I will keep you safe, warm and protected. You will be the boi that all boi's dream of."

With that He slams me with all His might. I yell out and His hand reaches up and covers my mouth strongly. His fingers work into my mouth, pulling as He fucks my hole soundly and with power of a Master. i am totally His boi, i can feel Him growing in me. He is coming closer i can sense it. His hand works my mouth, keeping me quiet as all His power slams my ass several more times and He shoots His sperm into my hole. My man cunt is filled with His juices to make me His total boi.

Slowly, His hand departs my mouth and begins rubbing my head, then my body. He stays in me a bit longer then pulls out. He stands and grabs my neck making me stand. We walk to His bedroom and He pushes me on the bed. He grabs several things from a drawer and climbs on the bed with me. He puts leather cuffs on my ankles and connects them. Then leather cuffs are put on my wrists. They are connected in front of me. Then a collar is put around my neck. He ties a rope to the ankle connection, loops it through the wrist and up to the collar. Then He takes a rope and attaches it to a collar He puts around His neck. i am now restrained loosely to Him. Our faces look at each other. His hand strokes my body and we begin to kiss, deeply and passionately. My restrained hands stroke His body, feeling the muscles in Him. We hug, kiss and stroke each other, feeling the love and passion that is driving us to be together.

"boi, we are now restrained together for the rest of the day. As I told you, I believe in the love of two Men and showing it to My boi and I expect Him to show it to Me. You have done so well. This is what our life will be, our passion together."

"Sir, i am so glad to be here, i want you near me, to touch me, to be in me"

"boi, I will."

We deeply kiss again, taking a strong hold of each other as His legs reach over me and bring our crotches together.

The morning turns into afternoon, as the shadow on the walls move a cross the room. i have lost all track of time, as we have spent hours in bed together, restrained to one another. At times we sleep at times we talk, but always touching, kissing and hugging. i would have never thought that my time with Sir would be like this. Can one Man show this much devotion to someone that shows me so much passion. At times He gets rough with me, holding me down with His strong legs or arm. He climbs on top of me, rubbing His always hard dick between my legs. i can't remember the last time my dick was soft. We have made a mess of each other with our pre-cum and sweat. He has even pissed on me a few times during the day. We are Men, loving each other without caring about what is going on in the outside world. my passions are so strong, that i could've cum long ago, and i know Sir knows that.

For the first time, He takes His hand and places it on my dick and begins to stroke it. Slowly, it feels so wonderful, as i arch my back to keep up with His strokes. He sits up and straddles my chest, with His strong dick in my face.

"Remember boi, I told you that My boi sperms also, and often. Well, it is your turn now. But as you do it, so will your Master."

With that He slams His dick into my mouth. i am pinned down where i can't reach Him, especially in my restraints. my legs are held together by the restraints on my ankles. He works my dick slowly, as He fucks my face. My tongue takes in His dick, His head and even explores His piss slit. He takes the back of my head in His other hand and pulls it up to His crotch. He begins to work my dick with more fever, as He fucks my face stronger and stronger. i begin to have trouble breathing and it is then that i realize that i am truly in His service, submitting to Him totally. He controls even my orgasms. My back tries to arch, but His weight keeps me pressed against the bed. i am getting so close.

"boi, you cum when I cum," he orders, but i can feel His dick getting close also. He works my dick stronger and faster. i moan as His dick fills my mouth, He starts to spasm as i know i am on the edge. i shoot first then in seconds His cum is filling my mouth. He slams to the back of my throat, pulling my head towards Him, as i shoot my load. i know it strikes His back and i shoot and shoot with a power i never knew i had.

The pace calms and i come to my senses. i can't believe what i have been through. It was wonderful and so powerful. i clean His dick with my tongue and He pulls out. He brings His hand around and i clean off my cum from His hand also. He rubs His hands over me as He sits over me, looking down at me. i take my restrained hands and reach up to Him pulling the collar that He has around His neck and bring Him to my lips. i give Him a deep kiss and He overpowers me and slams His tongue into mine. We kiss for a while, as He gropes my body, pulling and pinching as i struggle in my restraints.

When we are done, He releases all the restraints. i sit up with the help of His strong hands on my neck and we kiss again. He then grabs my still collared cock and balls, leading me out of the room. He takes me down the hall and down stairs. When we reach a stone room, i know i am in His dungeon. This is something that we had never talked about. i knew He loved BDSM, leather and all the gear. i just never thought He would have a dungeon. But it looked like a very complete dungeon.

He goes to a cupboard, pulling out several pieces of leather clothing. He hands me a pair of leather pants, shirt, vest, jacket and gloves. First He has me turn around and He puts a butt plug in my ass. It takes a bit, but soon i have it in. He then takes me to a table and has me lay down. He takes a syringe and puts it into my piss slit and puts lube in it. i have read enough to know that something was going in my dick. This was a new experience for me. He started to push in a rubber tube, it continues to go in and i could feel it inside me. Then it stopped and i had the urge to piss. He told me that i would and that i couldn't. He showed me the end of the hose and that it had a clamp on it.

Now i was helped off the table and ordered to put on all the leather. The hose from my dick was left hanging out the zipper. The pants were very tight and pressed against my bound cock and balls. He then handed me a pair of knee high lace up Doc Martin boots. i laced them very tightly. He took me to a mirror and there i was in full leather, tight pants, the tall white laced boots, the leather shirt covered with the leather vest, under the leather jacket, with my hand in leather gloves. i was getting hard and feeling that tube in my dick. i also felt the plug in my ass and could tell it was in there snuggly.

As i looked in the mirror, Sir came up from behind me and slid a full leather hood over my head. It covered my eyes, which were now sightless. There was a hole for my mouth. He laces the hood very tightly and then i heard a zipper down the back, followed by the snap of a lock on the collar. Then a gag was stuffed in my mouth, i could breath though it, but then it started to inflate and it filled my mouth. i felt a tiny bit of liquid coming through the gag and realized it has a tube to feed me liquids. This tasted like Sir's spit this time. i felt the gag strapped to my head, then another zip and i could feel leather coming down and covering the leather on my face. The leather smell was so strong this was one of the hoods in a hood. Now i was truly in full head to toe leather. Every opening in my body was plugged or gagged. i took my gloved hands and touched myself, feeling my leathered being.

Sir grabs and hugged me, pushing His crotch into my bound crotch. Then i felt Him take belts and secure my legs at the ankles, above and below the knees. i was told to lay back and He laid me on the floor. Slowly and with a comforting voice, i couldn't believe what happened next. Sir worked me into a full leather sleep sack. i was beginning to sweat in all this leather, the thought of another layer made me think of how hot i was to become. But still my hard, filled dick was straining at my pants zipper. i could barely hear the zips of the sack as they enclosed me. Then Sir took the straps and further secured me. Then there were more straps and i was strapped to the floor. He placed a pillow under my head for support.

There was fiddling at my crotch, as Sir opened the zipper of the leather pants and fished out my dick and balls. i could feel the gag in my mouth move around a bit and the breathing in that became harder, so i switched to my nose. i also sensed a strange taste coming from the hose that was leading to my mouth. As my mouth started to fill with my own piss, i heard Sir tell me that i could piss now. He laughed a bit as i tried to keep up with the running piss into my mouth. i was recycling myself now.

As the piss filled my mouth, i was jolted in my ass. Fuck, the plug in my ass was electric! And He wasn't starting easy with me. Another jolt and i almost choked on my own piss. i couldn't move as i was so securely strapped down. i was now feeling more helpless than i ever had.

Fuck, another jolt! And another. i was fucking my ass with the plug and there was no way i could get to my now hardening dick. As my ass was being fucked electrically Sir fiddle with my balls and i soon found them getting shocked also. The pain was becoming intense really fast. i was totally helpless to do a damn thing about it. i was being shocked over and over again. i could feel my dick growing, but the tube in me gave it a very different sensation.

Then Sir took His gloved hand and started to work my dick. Shit, He was going to make me sperm again! i had no choice in anything, i was His puppet to do as He fucking well wanted to. The shocks increased in frequency and power on my ass and balls. i was sweating like a pig now, cause of my activity and being in full leather. i couldn't stop this if i wanted to. Sir had total and complete control over me. He worked my dick faster and faster, rubbing His thumb over my head and i struggled in my bondage. Then i reached the point of no return, i had to shoot. He worked my dick harder and harder, the pulses in my ass and balls increased in speed. Then Sir reached for my nose and plugged it, i could not breath though the tube as i was sucking my dick. i was fucking helpless, in pain, struggling, sweating in full fucking leather, gagged, plugged, feeling my body against the restraints. It happened! i shot my load around the hose in my dick, fuck what a feeling! i was screaming in the gag as Sir continued the assault, as my cum felt like it just kept coming.

Then He let go. i heard Him say "good boi" to me through the hood. The electric shocks stopped, and i caught my breath. i wanted to hug my Master so for showing me this intense side of life, for caring for me so to show it to me. As i was just getting rested, the shocks started again, but bigger than before. i screamed into the gag, since it was now pure pain! i was helpless as i felt something entering the hose in my dick and i knew He was filling me up. i heard His voice through the hood.

"Fuck boi, you thought it was all fun, didn't you? boi, I am the Master and I will fucking use you to My amusement to the full extent. You better get use to it, because you are never leaving Me. I have captured my fucking Nazi fuck boi. I am going to leave now. You have several hours of this wonderful feeling of total fucking helplessness to enjoy. Remember, you wanted to serve Me. Now you are fuck boi. And I love it!"

Is He really fucking real about all this? What the fuck did i do? This is way more than i bargained for and so unlike what we did all day. The shocking was getting fucking painful, i could only scream in my gag, hoping that He really wasn't going to leave me this way. The cramping was beginning in my bladder, i wanted to fucking piss, even in my own mouth. i struggled by i was helpless, was i really becoming His total slave and was He going to keep me forever. Shit, i am getting hard again! This guy has to truly be my Master!

i am awaken again with the shocks that occur in my ass and around my balls. Sometimes they have been intense, other times just enough to let me know of my captive state. i have no idea how many hours i have sweated in this full leather cocoon. i sweat because i feel that my Master has turned up the heat in this room. Plus the activity my body goes through when i am being shocked. i have to admit that many times i have been hard, but unable to shoot my boi sperm. The cath in my dick gives a unique stimulation, but it is not enough to make me cum. Several times my bladder has been filled and kept that way for long times, then it is emptied as i drink it. i am unsure of how many times i have drank piss or was it water. It has been a random pattern of events during this time. i am sure it is night, for when we came to the room it was dark. How long i have been here, i have no idea.

i know that this is nothing what i imagined. And i keep thinking about after we arrived from the airport, how lusting Master was. We spent all those hours in the bed, tied together, kissing, hugging, fucking and sucking. That was moments that i never had with a Man that was into BDSM. And it was truly a great change. Then for Him to become almost cruel and sadistic in His nature, to torture me this way. Once or twice during my shock periods, i have wished i was released and catch a plane home. Then i tell myself that i will not give up. i want to serve this Master, i will take what He gives me and He will see how strong i am. Deep inside i know that i am enjoying this leather that encases me, the feel of the boots on my feet, the tightness of the straps that hold me in this leather sleep sack to the concrete floor, the layers of leather on my head, covering the inflated gag that fills my mouth with piss from time to time, the plug that self fucks my slave boi ass, the feeling of being out of control, controlled by this Skinhead Master.

As i near the point of shooting, the shock once again stop. But before my full bladder is allowed to empty in my mouth again, i feel something happening with my head, as weight presses on my chest. Could it be that Master is going to release me, finally! The gag is deflated as the zipper on the hood is pulled open. The gag is removed. i can see Master naked on my leather chest, as He brings His dick to my mouth. i open it proudly, and as He enters He lets go of His piss. It is strong and bitter, as it must be from Him holding it for a long time. i have gotten good at drinking quickly. Funny, but this time there is no shocking to accompany the drinking.

When Master is done, i lick His dick head and piss slit clean. He does not remove His dick and He begins to fuck my mouth. He works it harder, as my tongue works over Master's dick head and shaft. Still in full leather, Master is fucking the mouth of His slave boi. This is something i have been wanting since i was secured. It doesn't take long and He shoots His sperm into my mouth, where i savor it shortly, then let it slide down my throat to coat my insides with my Masters semen. i clean His dick head of any left over cum. He rubs my head with His hands, i see Him look at me. But He does not smile, or show any emotion. i am puzzled by this. He zips the hood back up, without the gag.

He begins working the straps and releases me from the leather sack. He helps me out and orders me to undress from the leathers. This is difficult since i can't see through the hood, but eventually get naked, except for the hood.

He leads me to a point in the room, where He secures my hands in a spread eagle position above me, my feet are restrained wide apart. My body is cool, as the sweat and nakedness takes over. It is strange going from total leather covered body, to naked body. i hear the buzz of the clippers as Master brings it to my body and begins to removed all the hair on my body. In this position He has full access. i am now truly becoming a skinhead boi, shaved and naked. After the clippers, He lathers my entire body and shaves it clean. i feel the air on my now naked cock and balls, as He removes the electro gear and shaves them. He pulls out the butt plug and shaves my ass. He then adds a parachute around my balls and secures it with chain to the floor, making me bend at the knees. Master removes my leather hood, the rush of dry air comes across my head and face. The scent of leather is gone for the first time in, what i think, is hours. With my balls secured, i am now at a height that Master takes clippers and removes all the hear on my head, then further shaves it with the razor.

This is the first time i have been able to fully see Him since before i was encased in leather. He is very emotionless in all that He does. He is naked before me, except in His tall boots. He works quickly and with precision.

When He completes my head, He puts a leather blindfold on me. My hands and feet are released and i am lead to the table. There i lay on my back, and am secured, with my arms to my side. He straps another gag in my mouth, this one holds down my tongue. i feel a bit messy with the shaving cream and stuff still on my body. With a rag He cleans my forehead. Then Master begins a type of torture i have never felt before. Sharp small pricks on my forehead, over and over again. There is no sound, just the pricks on my skin. They are methodical in their strikes and seem to go on forever. It is like the Chinese water torture that i have read about, although more maddening.

Finally He ends the torture, then speaks, "boi, time has come for Me to give you the rules of being My slave. Listen well, My boi, for I will not repeat myself. I like what I see in you so far boi, but you have much to learn. You are learning that I am going to train you hard, to make you the true Nazi slave boi you are. So that you serve this Nazi Master of yours with pride, servitude and dedication that I deserve and that you want to give Me. So from this moment on, I require that you no longer speak in my presence. My slave boi is silent. You have no say in anything that happens, since you put your full trust and life in My hands."

"I do expect your love and affection. You are most assuredly allowed to touch your Master at anytime, to show your love and devotion to Me at any time, with any part of My slave's body. you will sperm often under My command. As you will accept My sperm at any time. I have shaved you this time, but you will shave yourself each and every morning. I will do the areas you can't reach three times a week. You will keep your man cunt empty and clean at all times. As well as your slave mouth. This mouth that is now mine, is used only for My pleasure and release. You no long speak through it, do you understand?" i nod quickly.

"Good boi. When you nod, nod with conviction, so only one nod up and down for yes, once back and forth for no. If you fail on any of these commands, that will never be broken or rescinded, then you will be immediately put on the street. There is no slack in the Nazi family. you serve with pride and dedication at all times, not when it is convenient. Do you understand boi?" i nod again, this time is sharpness.

"Good boi. Now, it is morning and you need to get ready for today. you have lots to do before My friends arrive. I will lead you to the shower and you will clean yourself. Then I will put on your boots and collar. you will follow the instructions in the kitchen and prepare for My guests. These are important Men in My life. They are fellow Nazi's like Me. They will help in your training today by helping the teaching of Our Family and the Nazi meaning. you will do as They command, without hesitation or thought. you reflect upon Me boi, do you understand?" i nod again.

"boi, remember these rules, in time they will become natural for you. But don't slack, for we will not begin again." with that He releases me from the table. He walks me out of the room, still blindfolded and gagged. i feel the carpet under my feet, then it turns to cold tile. i am in the bathroom. He has me step up and i hear the shower water run. It is cold to start, but quickly warms.

"boi, removed the gag and blindfold, clean your naked slave body. When you're done, clean up the bathroom and report to the bedroom wear I will boot you." with that He leaves.

i remove the blindfold and gag, and enjoy the feeling of the hot water against my skin. It is a feeling like i haven't felt, for there is no hair between my skin and water. i clean myself quickly. i notice the enema tube attached to the shower, and take the motivation to use it on myself. Master wanted me clean, i strive to please Him. Funny, but a while ago i was seriously thinking of leaving, and i could right now. But now, i am filling myself with warm water to please my Master. As i finish showering, i dry myself and clean up the bathroom. There is a note on a black toothbrush for me to use. i brush. As i look in the steam covered mirror, i notice this black spot that seems to be on my forehead. i take the towel and wipe away the steam to see my naked head and something i can't believe. There on my forehead is a black swastika. The sharp stabbing, Master tattooed my head. i am panic stricken, how can i return to the outside world with this on my head!! i take the towel and rub at the swastika over and over, hard. But it won't come off. i can't believe this!

In my panic, i notice something about my dick, it is getting hard. i realize, i am truly in the service of this Master. He controls me totally. In our conversations, i have said i looked for a Master that took control. He is truly doing it. But i was supposed to leave after the weekend. Is He going to let me go? We need to talk about this, now!

i clean up the remaining things in the bathroom, then head to the bedroom. As i enter, Master is not in site. Then i am grabbed from behind and shoved to the bed. i struggle a bit, but Master gets my hands cuffed behind my back, pushing my legs open. He slams His dick right into my ass, as i scream. He grabs a pair of dirty underwear and slams it in my mouth. Then reaches under my chest and pinches my tits.

"boi, you've seen that sign of My ownership on your forehead, haven't you boi?", i nod yes. "boi, you wanted control, I have it. You want to talk about it don't you?", i nod again. "boi, you can't, you can't speak, you're My fucking cunt slave boi, that is all you need to know." With that, He slams my ass with His full power; this is not a gentle fuck by any means. i feel as if He is ripping off my tits, as i taste Him in the underwear that fills my mouth. He lets go of my tits for a moment and bring up my boots, shoving them in my face. i now smell the leather of those boots, those boots that enslave me. Soon, He shoots His load in His slave's ass. He sharply pulls out and rolls me over on my side. He takes my boots and puts them on my dick and begins to work them. The lug soles scrape my sensitive dick, hard and wanting to shoot. He squeezes the boots, up and down, up and down, over and over again. It is painful but erotic, fuck He has me, i am His tattooed Nazi slave boi, i can't deny that. Am i fucking insane?

He puts His head on my tits and bites one of my tits, then i shoot my load, a long time in coming, it feels powerful! i spasm over and over, the cum keeps coming. Master removes the now cum covered boots, lays them on my chest. He stands and leaves for a moment. When He returns, He takes the boots off my chest, roughly rolls me over and releases the hand cuffs. He rubs His hand on my skinhead, and for the first time, smiles at me again.

i stand, as He takes out His underwear. He hands me my boots, one by one, and i clean them with my tongue. Then i put them on, and He tightly laces them for me. i then kneel and lick His boots clean of the bits of cum that dropped from my ass. He slaps me on my ass and orders me to get to work in the kitchen.

i spend several hours in the kitchen preparing what is listed on the notes from Master. i feel funny at times, cooking and cleaning in my slave boi nakedness, but i feel comfortable with it at the same time. On occasions i see my reflection and that swastika on my forehead. It is strange, but i am now glad i have it. This Master is doing everything that i need to have done in my life. i am not sure how i would explain my new life to my family and friends. But all i know is that i am feeling more complete now than i ever have. So many of my friends would think that i am totally insane for continuing to explore with this Master. But when He smiled at me, after fucking me in the bedroom this morning, i could tell that He loved me. i know He truly is devoted to me, as i am becoming devoted to Him.

Suddenly, i hear Master shout for His boi. i have kept the kitchen clean as i have prepared. i quickly leave the kitchen and follow Masters voice to the dungeon. When i enter, i stop and hold my breath. What a vision to behold. My Master is in full black SS Uniform. The power that comes from that uniform. i just drop to my knees and kiss His tall black leather boots. From behind His back He brings His crop and it strikes me hard on my back. His leather gloved hand comes down on my head, strokes it, and then pulls my chin up to make me stand. i feel the strength and warmth from the wool of His uniform, against my shaved naked skin. He takes His mouth and slams it on mine, finally, we kiss again. His leather hands over my skinhead as His tongue explores His boi's mouth. Then the crop hits my ass, once, twice, then several times, as He kisses me deeply. Finally, the moment of passion has returned. i reach around and feel my uniformed Master in my arms as i bring Him closer. Then He releases the kiss, and kisses me on my tattooed forehead. He goes to a cabinet and brings forth my collar. Black leather with silver spikes on the outside. He puts it on tightly and locks it. A chain comes from the collar and drops to my cock and balls, which also go in a collar similar to the one around my neck. It too is tightly secured and locked.

He exits the room and i follow. In the living room, He points to a pillow placed in the corner. Snapping His fingers, i move to the corner quickly and kneel, the chain on my collar, pulling on my cock and balls.

Shortly, there is a knock on the door, and Master answers it. In come two handsome Men in full gray Nazi uniforms. The three Men, hug and laugh as they greet each other. As they finish, three other Men in uniforms arrive and the hugging and greeting continues. Then Master takes control of the moment.

"Gentlemen, I have some wonderful news. I have a slave boi dedicated to serving Me," they look and see me, naked, collared on my knees, with Masters tattoo claiming me as His. "As you see, he wears the symbol of Our Loyalty and Family." The Men all smile and congratulate Master. Master walks over to me, and strokes my head with His leather gloved hand, as i lay my head against the wool of His uniform pants.

"As you can see, he is devoted to Me, worships Me. But as you know, being a Nazi is for all. So, of course, My slave is Your slave. he will not bring shame on Me, I know that. he will serve You as he does Me, with pride, strength and dedication. I have asked You here today to help with My training of this slave. We must teach him the total Nazi way for he will become stronger with his knowledge of how to serve these Men that Master Him." With that, i just fall to kiss His boots.

"Gentlemen, have a seat. boi, serve us now." As they sit i go to the kitchen and prepare to serve these Nazi Masters of mine. What will my training entail today? i hope they are as good as Master. What is going on, how can i be feeling so proud, so strong. Then as i head out of the kitchen with the beers, i catch a glance at myself in the over window. i smile, for i am truly owned.

As i enter the living room, there before me are the Nazi Masters that i am going to serve today. As i approach each, on my knees with their imported German beers, i tingle with the thrill of serving such strong uniformed Men. Their wool uniforms are neither too tight nor too loose, neat, pressed and project the power they have. Their pants neatly wrinkle into their black full leather boots, boots that i crave to service. As i serve them, their stares are strong, piercing me, as they seek to explore my soul. i return the tray to the kitchen and return to the center of the room, kneeling.

Master instructs me to sit on the floor, back straight and to take in all the training that these great Masters are going to provide to me this day. He introduces the first Master to me, William. He approaches and i look from His booted feet up to His humbling stare. i bend over and kiss His boots, His leather gloved hand strokes my shaved head and passes over my tattoo of ownership. i listen as He gives me the history of the power of the Nazi's and the group that i am going serve. He speaks with conviction, knowing His way of life is what matters and will succeed to give Him the power He needs. On occasion He asks questions of me, but i do not speak, only nodding my head in reply. i find myself being wound up in His message, this is my training to enter a new life.

After what is more than an hour or more, He is complete. my mind is filled with so much information, it seems scattered. But i stay focused and remember what i have been taught. i am introduced to the second Master, Jason. i greet His boots with my slave lips. He shows no acceptance of that fact. He is too teach me Latin commands, so that Master may use an educated language with me. As i sit and listen He teaches me basics of this long forgotten language. Then He gives me commands, they are pounded into me, as i perform the commands. At times i forget, since there are so many, but i quickly learn. As He completes my training, i am lead to a closet. Master opens it and it is small, lined with black plastic. He tells me that i must be punished for my lack of follow through. While this was not a severe infraction, it must be dealt with. my hands are tightly cuffed behind my back, again Master is not gentle with me. He puts a gas mask with long breathing tube on me, with the eye glass allowing me to still see. i am put in the closet, sitting, my arms smashed against the wall, since the closet is so small. i watch as Master puts the tube to a connection in the wall and tapes it secure. The door is closed and i am in darkness. Then before me a slight orange glow. And i feel heat being pumped into the closet. With the plastic and small space, i know that i am going to be getting pretty warm. The cuffs bite into my wrists, as i begin to sweat. Then the air in the hose to my mask is cut off. i struggle to breath, being silent in doing so. i bang against the walls at times. The air returns. It is repeated several times, me sweating more and more as the heat gets intense in the small space.

Time passes, the struggle of breathing continues. Then liquid fills my mask and i drink quickly in able to breath and not drown. The taste is salty and beer like. i know that they are pissing into their slave. i can't stand how hot it is. The heater turns off after a good thirty minutes must have passed. All this time, i have been struggling with my breathing, either by it being cut off, or by liquid filling the hose. Sweat pours down my body, out of my rubber covered head. i feel my skin slide along the plastic on the walls and floor. Finally i notice that my breath has not been cut off for a while, nor have i drank my Master's piss. This silence in activity lasts, and lasts. The heat is stifling, as the humidity builds from my sweat. Then i feel that i must piss. But i can't do it in this closet. i must wait for Master to release me. That too adds to the misery that i am feeling. So little bondage holds me here, but i am trapped.

Time passes slowly, as it always does when i am in bondage. Finally, i see a sliver of light, as it widens and Master opens the door. The cool fresh air strikes me like a sharp smack across my skin. Master grabs me by collar and pulls me out. i am lead to the back door and instructed to go outside, like the dog i am, and piss. Master opens the door and His boot kicks me out. i crawl to the grass and trying to relax to make the effort to relieve myself. Here i am in the outdoors, the true Nazi slave dog, pissing. i finally am able to soften my dick so that i can pee. It feels wonderful to release my bladder. i then crawl back to the door and knock. i am let back in, the collar grabbed and led back to the center of the room.

The third Master stands before me, His boots showing my reflection of my sweat dried body. As with the other Masters, i show my total respect and put my lips to his boot leather. Master Alex removes His gun from His holster. This was something that i had not noticed them having when they arrived. But i admit that i was not paying attention to that. He shows it to me closely, a chrome hand gun that shines and reflects His blond hair and face. He tells me how i will worship this weapon of personal power. It will protect me, as well as my Master and all that i serve. i will learn to use one so that i can protect my Master from the evils that are in our everyday society. He orders me to kiss the barrel. i do, feeling the cold stainless on my lips. i pull my head back, Master Alex grabs it and holds the gun to my lips. "Lick it slave", He commands strongly. my tongue touches this cold metal, making it warm. i cover the barrel. He instructs me to worship it like i do my Masters boots. i do so, and i am over come with the power this has over me. i lick the trigger section, the handle and even the hole that the killer bullet comes out of. Then Master takes the gun and shoves it in my mouth. i suck on it, like my Masters dick. i have no idea if the gun is loaded, cocked. It could go off without a warning and i would be a slave to no one. This is getting more intense and His gloved hand holds my head close to His booted legs and i continue to worship the gun with my mouth. The cold metal is now warm with the mouth of this Nazi slave.

He then orders me to cease, i do so quickly. i am ordered to put my face on the floor and lift my ass to the air. i do so quickly, then i feel the slippery hand gun make it's way, up and down my ass crack. Master tells me how i will be fully devoted to the guns They use, with that He pushes it into my ass. Slowly, He begins fucking my ass with the gun. It can't go in far, but it is big enough to open my hole fairly wide. i feel my cock growing, pulling on the chain and leather that secure it to my collar. Master's booted foot comes down on my neck, grinding my face into the floor. All this time He instills in me how much of a slave i am, how i am theirs to do at they please, total slave, being fucked by a gun. Another Master comes before me and shoves His boots in my face. i start licking and sucking on them, to the praise of my Master. Soon, i am done with the boots and the other Master takes the gun out of my ass. He pulls me up by the collar and pushes the gun into my slave mouth, to clean it. i taste myself as i thoroughly clean the gun.

He hands me the gun and instructs me how to handle it. What the parts are and how it would work. Then He tells me to point it at Him. i don't want to do so, but i do with hesitation. As i do, the others pull their weapons and they are pointed straight at me. Master Alex laughs, "slave, you have learned that any attempt to harm a Master and you will die." With that He rips the gun out of my hand and kicks me with His boot in my stomach. i curl to the floor in deep breaths to regain my breathing. The others laugh at this slave as they return their weapons.

The next Master approaches and i kiss His boots, as He is introduced. John is the most muscular of the group, filling His uniform tighter than the rest. He orders me to stand and i am dragged by my collar to the dungeon.

There, exercise gear has been set up. The dungeon door slams shut as just Master John and i are alone in the room. He pushes me on the treadmill and starts it quickly. i am walking quickly to keep up, as the chain from my collar pulls on my balls. He talks firmly to me how He will train my weak pitiful slave body into something that any Master would be proud to own. That even a Nazi slave must show power, strength and health. This is not a short walk, it is long and He continually speeds it up. The incline is also increases, as my legs work harder and my balls are tugged even more. After a good half hour, He stops me and i step off the treadmill. He hands me a pair of gloves and i put them on. That is followed by some 10 pound hand weights. Those are then taped on my hands with duct tape. There is no way for me to release them. He shows me various routines to perform, stressing my muscles in places i never knew. After the third routine, He puts a pair of tight tit clamps on my tits. He explains that working hard, with pain increases my training abilities, making me want to work harder and faster to complete my workouts.

He is right, but i work harder to improve for my Masters also. i again work up a sweat, with a vigorous workout. When i move, the tit clamps or the chain on my balls reminds me of my slavery. After a long time and many repetitions, i am laid on a workout bench and start new routines. After several, He stops me with my hands in the air, extended over me straight up. He instructs me that i am going to hold them for ten minutes. This seems easy to start, but after only a few moments, my arms begin to strain. Then He reaches down and pulls the tit clamps off my tits. In pain i drop my arms, He yells at me to lift those hands again. i do so quickly, as the pain continues to boil in my tits. He instructs me that i will now hold them that way for 15 minutes. And if i drop them again, He will add one minute each time, until i am completed.

i feel His stare at me, i don't dare look. My arms are stressing under the weight. They wobble back and forth, but i focus my attention at making the goal. "Five minutes", He tells me. Shit, it seemed like ten to me. Then i hear a whoosh and His belt comes crashing across my chest. My first reaction is to protect myself, but i return to my mission and keep my hands in the air. The belt crashes across my chest time and time again. i feel my skin lighting on fire. How much more can i take of this. The beating stops and i continue to struggle. "Ten minutes", He reminds me. Then cold water is splashed on me, taking the burning chest and stomach to a new level or sensitivity. But i keep the weights held high, as my arms struggle and shake. Finally He tells me to drop them, fifteen minutes is completed. He tells me good boi and places His boot on my chest for me to kiss. i thank Him for the training.

As i am kissing His boot, Master and the other Men enter the dungeon. John tells my Master how good i did. i feel very proud for what i have accomplished so far. i have not failed Master in nearly all that i have been given to do. He comes to me and orders me to stand. i do so quickly, as the other Masters remove the weights, gloves, as well as the collar and chain. Master stands before me and speaks:

"slave, you have done well today. you have learned that your training will include many different aspects of total ownership by Myself and the Nazi Men here. It will be difficult, stressful and sometime brutal in what it teaches you. Through it all, you will only accept what you are trained. you will never question, only agree with and take in what you are given. you will become the best man that there is on earth, while still being only a slave that serves an even higher Man. Now it is time to bring your training to its conclusion for the night." He said night, how long have i been training, as i start to trace things, it must have been hours.

Master goes to a closet and returns, He hands me a gray full Nazi uniform, complete with boots. i can't believe this. He instructs me to put it on. i kneel and lick His boots with the full force of my tongue, His leather gloved hand lightly, somewhat coldly strokes my head. i stand and put on the uniform. It seems to fit so well, as the wool on the pant legs climbs my skin. A cotton shirt is buttoned, and tucked into the pants. i tuck in my hard dick and zip the pants up. A wonderful leather belt with metal buckle with swastika complete His part of the uniform. i take the boots and lick them, taking in the wonderful smell and slide my feet into them, tucking my pant legs in tightly. The coat follows, buttoning and snapping the belt. Leather gloves and hat complete this great gift from my Master.

"slave, show your appreciation to all these great Masters of yours." i kneel and begin licking and kissing their boots. How powerful it is to be in full uniform at their boots. i can't believe this is my life now. How lucky i am. i forget the tattoo on my head until i see it in the reflection of one of the boots i service. i hear a zipper and then feel wetness on my back, i look around to find Master pissing on my uniform. i can't believe this and feel hurt. Then another Master starts pissing on me, followed by another. i feel so humble as they piss on my uniform and it soaks to my skin. They laugh at me as this once proud slave is made even lower. My hands are grabbed and roped is being wrapped around them and my wrists, tightly. Then my elbows are tightly secured, throwing my chest out. i am stood up and a hood covers my piss soaked head. The leather fills my nose with a great smell, as my dick grows against the wool of my uniform pants.

The hood is tightly laced with the gag filling my mouth and the blindfold keeping my sight in darkness. i am lead to a small platform and told to stand on it. After doing so, my booted legs are tied tight at the ankles and knees with rope. i am helpless as i feel the wool and leather against the skin on my legs. my cock is fished out of the pants and tied off with a small leather thong. i feel something go around my neck. Tightly it pulls me to my tip toes, somewhat choking me. It is a thick rope, i can tell that much, pushing on the side of my head and somewhat crushing my Adam's apple.

The blindfold is removed and i am shocked by the site. The uniformed Masters are all before me with their guns pulled. Master Alex holds a rope that leads to the noose around my neck. i am in total bondage, gagged standing on a platform that Master John holds another rope that will pull it out from beneath me. This is not what i had expected at all. i can't believe i let myself get into this situation. i trusted Master so much and He has been growing more evil with every moment. Yet, i am so damn hard, i wanted someone to control me like this, i know this is what i need.

Master speaks, "slave shit, you are now in the position to control the rest of your life. you have come here of your own free will, you have seen what your life will be. you will be fulfilled with the service to Me. Nothing in your life will matter, you will worship and devote your entire existence to me. Now is the time for you to make a choice, is this the life you want. Think of the position you are in and think wisely of your answer. i will not influence you in anyway. For it is only you that will decide your fate. Will you be nothing on the face of the planet, to rot to dirt, or will you become a Nazi slave serving the most powerful Men on this planet. Decide now, slave."

With that they draw their guns higher. i feel the tightness of the rope against my skin, as i struggle a bit. i don't make a sound, feeling the piss wet uniform on my skin, how heavy it is, how great the wool feels. i look before me and see these powerful Men, controlling every piece of my life. They might kill me right here, or they will let me serve them. i smell the leather covering my head, tight, the gag filling my mouth, full. my hands behind my back in leather gloves, wearing full leather boots on my slave feet, the rope pulling tighter against my neck as the stool starts to wobble a bit. i am getting harder as the thong tightens around my cock and balls. Shit, i could've have never dreamed this, i am in His control, i am His i am a Nazi slave. i nod yes.

The stool is pulled from under my feet and i struggle in my bondage as the noose pulls tightly against my neck...i find it hard to breath. Someone's gloved hand grabs my dick and starts working it, over and over as i struggle and move swinging. i am helpless, i am having a hard time breathing, the wool, leather, piss, rope, those Masters before me, i am theirs, i am theirs....i shoot with the power i have never felt before, i shoot over and over. Someone grabs my legs as i feel faint and slowly pass out.

i wake to find myself naked strapped down on my chest to a table. i am in a leather hood but a piss gag fills my mouth. Before is

Master naked, as is the other Masters.

"slave, you have chosen wisely. As your reward, We initiate you to Our Kingdom." With that His dick slams into my mouth as another Master slams His dick into my greased ass. i am now the total slave i dreamed to be. They take turns fucking me in my holes. At times they piss on me or in me, they shoot their cum on me and in me. i am their total slave. This sex last for hours, they rest and fill my mind with what my life is going to be in the future. They beat me with their belts, hands and even boots. They use toys to keep my ass and mouth filled when not in use. When they are finally exhausted, they gather their uniforms and leave. i am alone in the room. Totally used. i fall asleep.

i wake to find Master naked, releasing me. i move my abused body slowly, bring the blood back to the various parts that have been unused for the night or day, or how ever long it was. He shows me a silver chain with a gold lock. The lock has a Nazi eagle on it, with a swastika carved on a shield. Master takes the chain and locks it around my neck. He leads me from the dungeon and to the bathroom. There He allows me to shower, shave and release myself. The water feels so wonderful as it washes away hours of sweat, piss, cum and Man scents. It washes away memories of how i became a slave this day gone by.

When i am done, Master dries me with a towel, leads me to the bed room. He climbs in bed and orders me to follow. He grabs my head and deep kisses me. i melt, this is the Master i want to serve, He has returned. My arms go around Him and i take Him in me, wanting Him in me for my life. Our warm bodies mesh and stay together. For hours, once again, it is only us in the bed, as the sun moves across the wall with the shadows being our only time.

The day turns into night. He fucks me at times, and at times He allows me to shoot my load. We let this life cum mix between us, bringing us to complete one. The touch of His powerful hands against my shaven body, my stroke of His muscles, i want to serve Him with every fiber i can. Then He gets up and goes to the closet. He opens it and begins to put out the clothes i wore from the airport. i know what this means. Time has come for me to return. He sits next to me, "slave, as promised, you are going to be released to return to your temporary home. i want you to return to serve me. That is why you wear that chain. You will wear it until you get home. In your mail box you will find an envelope with key to unlock it. Remove the chain and keep it until you return. i don't want you to be causing commotion with such a thing. As of right now, your silence it no long needed. You are free to speak slave. i love you my slave and will have no one but you serving me." With that, He kisses me with the most powerful kiss i have ever felt. i begin to tear up a bit as He lets go of the kiss. i don't know what to say, how to say it, or even if i should say it. All i can say, "Master, thank you for discovering your slave."

i get dressed as Master does. He looks so wonderful in his skinhead uniform. Deep inside me, this is the moment that i really didn't expect to have. The moment where i truly wish i was not free to go. Yes, all those times in the dungeon, serving the many Masters, the cruelty, pain and suffering way beyond what i knew i could do. But i did do it, and this Master proved me to myself, that i can indeed serve, proudly. He orders me to clean my face before going. i look in the mirror as i enter the bathroom and find the swastika tattoo, or what i thought was a tattoo is gone. i stare, touching my forehead, wondering where it went. How i hated Him in the beginning for doing such a thing. But now i know how much comfort it gave me. It was like a hug from Master, His touch to me, always to be there.

As we drive to the airport, there is mostly silence. While i have gone through so much in the past three days, i am speechless. i know He owns me, with that feeling, i am more complete than i have ever been in my life. We sit at the gate, me in my snug jeans,

Fred Perry navy shirt, and tall Doc Martins, proudly showing my devotion to my Master. As they call my row number, i get up and kneel before Him, kissing His Docs, then i kiss Him deeply with passion that i have never known and know that will be in my life with Him forever.

When i arrive home, i go straight to the mail box. i find the letter with the key to His collar. i take a pen out of my pack and cross out the address, writing "Return to Sender", and drop it in the mail out box. i head to my apartment to plan my return to Master and my Nazi slave boi life.

my time with my Nazi Master has been beyond my imagination. The first weekend told me a great deal about myself as well as what my future was going to be in his service. i wore his collar and lock without fail during the two months it took to move me to his home. my training was intense, non stop and immersed me into the Nazi lifestyle that he wanted me to crave. Through it all, i knew that i was making him proud for accepting me into his Family. His friends all were jealous of him for having a boi like me. But they helped with my training. In the end the collar and lock were removed and i was tattooed by Master with an eagle and swastika on my chest. After the tattoo was done, Master approached me. i looked down at his white laced black Rangers and kneeled. His leather gloved hand stroked my shaved head, as he pulled me to the crotch of his bleached denim. i could feel his hard dick through it and wanted so much to pull it out. He slammed the back of my neck with his open hand, forcing my face in his crotch. His knee came up and knocked my jaw, as his boot found it's place in my crotch. i moaned, and again his hand slammed my neck, harder and with a Master's force. He ground his boot into my dick, not much protection was offered by the gray BDU's that i wore. Holding my neck he forced my face in his crotch so tight i could barely breathe.

i felt handcuffs applied to my wrists, as my hands were behind my back. The tattoo artist must have applied them since Master never let go of my neck. As i chewed on Master's denim, i felt it beginning to get moist. Master was pissing, i worked hard to suck as much as i could from his pants. i was pulled so close to him, i could feel it run down his leg on my bare chest. i sucked as hard as i could, but i was missing most of it. He stopped pissing and kicked me backwards. i awkwardly fell to the floor, landing hard on my shoulder. With my arms cuffed behind my back, it was difficult to move around. i felt Master's piss strike my bare skin. i looked up to see he had removed his dick from his denim and was showering me. He ordered me on my back, and as much as it hurt, i did so right away. He aimed his piss right at the new tattoo, followed shortly by the artist. Then Master took his boot and ground the piss into my freshly altered skin. i could feel those lug soles tearing my skin as Master moved his boot from top to bottom. After, he raised it to my lips, and i began cleaning the soles with my tongue. i tasted the piss and ink. He slammed his boot down next to my right ear and smiled at me. Dropping to his knees, he bent down and slammed his tongue into my mouth. In my eyes i saw my shaved Skin Master dominate me with his kiss; i was wearing his tattoo for life. He loved his Skin slave boi, and i loved him. We rolled roughly on the floor as the artist would take a turn in kicking me when i was moved close to him. All the while, Master never let our lips separate. Our breathing filled the room, the squeaks of our boots and the power of my Master rolling around with cuffed slave.

That night took eight months to reach. That is when i was giving full information in Masters life. i had been helping him in his design business in Denver. One day he notified me that we were going to be moving. Master had been appointed the Director of a National movement promoting the rights and destiny of the Gay Federation Reich. i would be employed in this group in designing marketing and promotional materials.

By then, my communication with my friends had all but been

ended, and i only talked on the phone with my family. Now it was time to end that. i notified them that i was on a special assignment and would not be in communication again for a very long time. Master loved that phone call, for he was holding a gun to my head when i did it. He knew i didn't need that, but he loved the power that it gave him.

Since my becoming Master's slave, my shooting skills are excellent; i can light a match from 100 yards. Master and i often converse in Latin, and i have read Mien Kampf several times. i have lost 40 pounds, but have another 10 to go. i work out everyday, with my running up to six miles. i sweat a great deal, Master likes to see me sweat. To him, it proves my loyalty to him and the Reich. We have settled in a great home provided by the Reich. Master and i have made some changes to the home, including a wonderful dungeon that he designed and i constructed over the past 7 months we've been here. While i love serving Master, his new position has not allowed us the time we once have. i was surprised to learn that this Reich is all homosexual men, that believe that the order and guidance of Nazism will help bring more rights to us all. All in the complex know of my service to Master, and i have given instruction to other slaves that have been brought into service of others in the Reich. While i got to know the others that helped train me in Denver, none of them came to our new home in South Carolina. i lost touch with them and it was for a good reason. i think one of them was starting to get me to believe that my Master was not good for me. i know he wanted me to serve him. But as i promised my Master, only death would take me away from him.

When i agreed to visit Master so long ago, i would have never guessed that my life would change so much. But it has change for the better. i am so fulfilled in my life. While i am a total slave to Master, i am strong, educated, and have a purpose in all that i do. i have spent days in a cage, with only water to survive as part of my training. But i have also spoken to groups about our cause, developed successful materials that are seen around the world. We have marched around the country, often with hated audiences to our cause. But if they could only see that what we strive for is pure freedom for all homosexual men. Most of what Master does is beyond my knowledge and we often have visits by the law checking up on us. But inside i know that Master would never lead a group that would not exist for the sole reason of make our life better.

As i woke in the morning, i was somehow looking back on how i got to the point in my life that i was so happy. i turned my hooded head to see Master laying next to me. He had tied me to him two days ago, and we haven't left the bed. i have learned that these long moments of love, passion and sex always led to an intense period of pain and suffering for me. i always got fucking hard just thinking of that torture coming. Master knew it and made me shoot my load over and over to make sure i wouldn't be tempted to do so when i was being abused.

i wanted to start to kiss my Master, but he had inserted the gag last night before falling asleep. He also secured my hands behind my back. i did move closer to feel him. Slowly Master stirred and i saw one eye open, there was his smile and he reached down to find my dick growing between his legs.

"Hail boi," he said as he reached around me and hugged me. i moaned in the gag, so wanting to hold him in return. Just then the telephone rang. Master swore, and then rolled over to answer it. Being cordless he took it into another room and left me lying helpless on the bed.

Several minutes later, Master returned, jumping on the bed, straddling me.

"Fuck boi, i have to head out of town. Crisis in Chicago that needs my attention. i'm sorry but i won't be leaving you with any scars for a while," Master says as he is undoing the ropes. "But you have your work to do, it is on the computer. Also, you'll have to walk to town to get your food. No ride today." When he is done releasing my bondage, he gets up and heads to the shower. i know it must be important that he hurries, for we do none of the normal morning routine. i fix him some breakfast and have it waiting while i put out his clothes for his travel. As he gets dressed, he unlocks the hood and i store it in the drawer next to the bed. He puts on a pair of black BDU pants, his 14 hole Rangers, with ladder lacing, black Fred Perry and his black bomber. i run my hand across his head, as he heads to the kitchen. As he eats, i shower and get ready. After shaving and showering, i put on my gray BDU's, Fred Perry, 14 hole Rangers and white braces. Master grabs his briefcase and comes to me. He grabs his slave by the shirt chest, pulling me close and fucking rapes my mouth with his. i grab him and pull him into me, arching my legs around his. i know i am going to miss my Master's kiss. He pulls back, brings up a large wad, and spits it in my mouth. He smiles and slaps my face. He goes to the door, turns, "Seig Heil, slave."

i stand at attention, raise my right hand, "Seig Heil, Master!". As he walks out the door, i swallow his load and head to the kitchen to clean up.

The walk to town is only four miles, on a long stretch of country road. i walk for Master as he does not allow me to drive. He might be purchasing me a motorcycle next year, but for now, unless he drives, i walk. There is a slight chill in the spring air, so i am glad i grabbed my bomber and gloves before heading out. Once in a while when i walk this road a redneck will honk and yell fucking shit at me. i just flip them off. They are more talk than action, knowing that the Reich would destroy them if they touched me. As i walk forward, i hear a car approaching behind me. i think nothing of it, until i notice it is slowing down. i turn and see it is a cop car. They slow, pass me and pull over, blocking my path. i wonder what the fuck to they want. On occasion they have harassed other members of the Reich, and then let them go. Mostly just verbal abuse, they seldom do much more. i think they are pretty chicken of the power we have.

i stop in my tracks as the driver and passenger doors open in unison. Out steps two cops, both in the navy uniform, jacket, boots and such. While they look good in their uniforms, they would never look better than Master in his black SS uniform. They shut their doors, the driver walks towards me, pulling on his gloves as he approaches.

"Boy, what you doing out here?"

"Sir, headed to the store for my dinner." i reply politely. Master has trained me that everyone is a Sir, for i am a lower form of man.

"You're from that Order back there, aren't you Boy?."

"Sir, i am from the Reich. You know who i am, who i serve. What can i do for you, Sir?"

He looks back at his partner, "Yup, you're right, it is him." As he turns back around with a chuckle, he slams his fist in my stomach with no warning. i keel over as the air escapes my body. "I don't need no back talk from you boy."

"Yes Sir." barely comes out of my breathless bent body.

His booted foot comes up to strike me in the balls; i see it coming and push my arms out to knock him back. He falls to the ground, missing me. His partner runs to help him out. Before i figure out what i have done, his partner has grabbed me and thrown me to the ground. i know that i am not suppose to fight another higher Man, but i am trained to protect myself. These guys seem to want to harm me and i don't know why. They will not win.

One of them works my hands behind my back, struggling to get his cuffs around my wrists. i fight with all the might and muscles that Master has built in me. The other is standing and kicks me a couple of times in my side to get me to submit. One of the cuffs is tightened and latched on my wrist, but the cop struggles with me to get the other one on. Then i hear it, the click of a gun being cocked. i feel the cold against my neck and i freeze. The toe of one of the cop's boots fills my mouth gagging me as the other cuffs easily slaps around my gloved wrist. They both laugh as they finally subdue me.

"Suck on that boot boy." says the cop as he slowly moves the gun up and down my neck. "Guess you ain't so fucking smart now, are ya?"

i taste the polish and dirt that covers the leather and sole that fill my mouth. The other cop stands and kicks me with all his might, "Fucking don't fight the law, asshole!" i feel my booted feet flail around as the settle from the stinging kick. i try to yell at him but the boot fills my mouth.

i hear the cock of the gun returned and removed from my skin. The boot comes out and i am helped up by the cops. The driver cop turns me to him and brings his face an inch from mine. i try to see those eyes of his behind those mirrored sunglasses. He stares me down, no expression on his face. i hear the latch of their car trunk unlocked. But i don't move my sight from this fucking asshole cop. Then there is a slight up turn to his lips and he whispers, "Such a fucking waste."

He hurls a large gob at me, landing on my cheek. As it slides down my face, i stare him directly, take out my tongue and bring in as much as i can into my mouth. i notice a slight flinch from him, and i smile. He turns me to the car and drags me there.

In the trunk is a gym bag of workout gear. The second cop fumbles through it and finds a pair of socks. He brings one to my mouth, balling it up. As he moves it in, i smell it, nasty, must have been used for days. He shoves it in as i struggle a bit. He grabs a role of athletic tape and wraps it around my mouth and head, securing the gag sock tightly in. They push me in the trunk head first. my head lands in the gym bag and i struggle to move it out of the way but am not successful. They load my feet in and wrap tape around them also. The trunk slams shut and i am in darkness. i start to smell the fucking ripe shoes that are in the bag and can't get my head out of it. The car starts and we are moving. As it starts to get warm in the trunk, i know that it is at least an hour to the county jail. That is, if that is where i am being taken. Not sure what these fuckers are up too, but in the end, they will not like the consequences.

i'm sweating like a pig in this trunk. The odor from the gym bag seems to get stronger as it gets warmer. But i've dealt with worse with Masters PT clothing after he works out. Sometimes he wears it for weeks without cleaning it. He'll put me in the closet in full bondage with his old shorts over my head and let me sweat it out for a few hours. i have come to love Master's smell. But this is fucking cop smell and it is not as good as Master's. As i am thinking this, i am slammed against the tail of the car as the speed rapidly increases and i hear the muffled sound of the sirens. This is fucking nuts; they are chasing someone down or running to a call with me in their trunk! As they turn the corners at high speeds i am helplessly thrown around this trunk, slamming into the stuff that lies around. One point something punches my stomach. It is like getting beat up, but no one is doing it. The only good point is when they stop fast and i roll on my back and get my face out of their stinking sweat gear. After the last fast stop the car is still and the sirens go dead. i am able to keep my face up, getting the warm but somewhat cleaner air to breath. But lying in the position, the cuffs cut into my wrists. i eventually have to give up and fall back into the bag.

Time seems to pass by without any action or sounds from the outside world. i wonder what the person they are helping or arresting would think if they knew this skinhead was in the trunk of the cops. While i am never sure how long i've been in the trunk, it does seem like hours before the car starts again and i feel the movement. Thankfully it is not in pursuit again.

The car comes to a stop again and i can faintly hear the doors slam shut. i am thinking this is where i get to see where they are taking me. The trunk pops open, but i am surprised that i am not blinded by the daylight. It is only because we are in the garage. They spit on me then pull something over my head. i hear the damn tape again as it is sealed around my neck. They release my feet and drag me out of the trunk.

i hear some noise of people, phones ringing, etc. i am pushed against the wall. Someone roughly frisks me down. He seems pretty interested in my crotch and ass, squeezing tightly, chuckling as he hears the moan through the hood i am wearing. i hear a whisper through the bag on my head, "i fucking hate you gay Nazi's!" With that he slams his fist in my gut.

i kneel over in pain and i hear his boots walk away. Someone grabs my arms and moves me along. i'm taken down some halls, hearing heavy doors slam. i am made to stand alone, i feel something slender pushing to the side of my face.

"Boy, if you wanna live, you won't move when i remove these cuffs. i'd hate to have to think that i need to pull the trigger."

i then get a clue to the gun that is pressing into my skin through the hood that i am wearing. The cuffs are removed and i get a second to rub my wrists. i am sharply grabbed by those wrist. my bomber is removed and my arms are shoved down sleeves that have a cold surface. i think it is leather. There are no ends to the sleeves. The jacket is strapped up my back and my arms pulled around my side. i realize that i am in a straight jacket. They secure it very tightly and i struggle to get out of it. i am pushed and slam into a padded wall. Loosing my balance i fall to the floor, which is also padded. The roughly grab my ankles and secure them together, then my knees. i feel the boot of one of the guys rolls me back and forth letting me know how helpless i am in the leather and bondage. Another boots steps on my head and grinds my face into the mat that covers the floor. Then i am kicked a few times, i heard the door slam. It sounds heavy and metal. Then i only hear my breathing in the bag that covers my head. i can't hear anything else. There no outside sound. i am very alone. i struggle to right myself, but it isn't easy. i finally find a wall and get myself to sit up, leaning against the wall. i try to work my arms out of the sleeves. But it is no use. Eventually i give up and realize that they got me. The fucking cops got me in their control. i don't know what they want out of me, but they aren't going to get it. Eventually the compound will notice i'm missing and contact Master. i know he will be upset and start looking for me right away.

What the fuck are these cops doing to me, why did they pick me up now? Then i remember what Master and i did a couple of months back. He was testing me, my loyalty and service to him. We were in Atlanta; he was speaking to a conference. One night we had gone out for dinner and were walking in the gay area of the city. This younger kid started flipping us shit, calling us racist and killers. We are only racists when it comes to wanting equal rights for all gay men, no matter the color. It was late; i think around 11 or so at night and this fuck head wouldn't leave us alone. Master ordered me to try to talk to the punk and set him straight.

i stopped turned and went over to where he now stood after following us for a while. i think he was a bit startled about that. He looked at me, taking in my 14 hole Rangers and following up my bleached jeans and braces. He leaned against the wall as i stopped and spread my feet slightly apart. my hands when behind my back and i stared at him for a moment. "What the fuck is your problem?" i asked him, never letting his eyes out of my sight.

"You guys kill people, that is so fucking wrong."

"Why do you say we kill, you see us do it?"

"i read the internet. Those laces in your boots mean you hate niggers, you're white power."

"You're white, so why should that matter."

"i'm for everyone, even though i'm white."

"But you just use the word nigger, asshole."

"i was making a statement," i rolled my eyes as he tried to compensate for his stupidity.

"Plus i'm not the one that is a racist skinhead."

"i'll tell you about who i am. i serve that Man over there and his followers. We are a party of gay men that are fighting to achieve equal right for all gay men. We don't care about color, race, or background. We believe in the power of Man and enforcing that power for all."

"What the fuck, you're gay? God damn faggot and racist. How can you do that?"

"You're in the gay part of this city, why is that? You out cruising for some cock to suck?" that pissed him off. i could tell he was getting anxious of the situation. Master was off in the distance watching this conversation. The guy looked over at him, as his fists were balling up. i knew he wanted to take a swing at me, but he was hesitant of Master standing near by.

"I'll fuck your ass, skin ass." he snarled at me, taking a more aggressive stance.

"Tell you what boy. i'm going to turn around and we'll move on. You can remember this night as the night that a gay skinhead did kick your ass until you were pleading for your life."

He was speechless as i turned and headed towards Master. When i was at Master's side, he looked at me, grabbing my tit and twisted it. He pulled me in front of him. Staring me directly, he was serious in his tone. "We're going to beat and rape that ass. My boi doesn't take his shit. You are going to take the lead boi, go over there and show him the power of the Reich."

my heart was pound, i have never been aggressive like this. Master and his buds had taught me combat and self defense, but i had never used it. But he wanted me to and i had to. i only hoped that in the end i would make him proud.

i walked over the punk again, he hadn't moved. i think he was trying to prove he was a Man, his first mistake. i stood before him, crossed my arms and cleanly spit in his face. He started to move his fist towards me, but i blocked and landed a sharp hook to his chin. He screamed and grabbed his face. i could see a small trickle of blood coming from his lips. i had made a guy bleed. i was in control of the situation. i was beginning to feel some power, something my Master had warned me that i would feel someday as his boi.

The punk looked at me and tried to get another punch off, but i kneed his balls, he screamed in pain, and then i slugged his side. As i did, Master reached and grabbed his collar. i didn't realize that he had come up behind me. He grabbed me also and dragged us to the alley that was near by. Now i wasn't sure if he was pissed with me or what was going on.

The alley was dark and somewhat damp from the rain yesterday. He threw the punk against a trash can and pushed me into him. i turned to him as i found my balance, "boi, finish the fucker off, no mercy. You're a member of the Reich show him your power."

i turned to him, feeling this power that i have achieved. i took my steel toed rangers and started kicking this slug that was laying on the wet trash. A perfect position for him. He was started to beg for mercy, but that just made me want to hurt him more. Master came in and started kicking him also. His 20 hole steel toes just laid into him harder and harder. The thud of the leather and soles hitting his body was intoxicating. Master reached down and brought the guy to his feet, he could barely stand. Master fished some cord out of the trash and wrapped it around the guy's neck and to a pipe on the wall. he was now straggling himself as he fell down. Master tied is hands off behind his back and started slugging the guy. The leather of Masters gloved hands made a smacking sound that i loved to hear. Then i wanted my turn, i actually pushed Master off him and started striking the guy on my own. i hesitated for a moment when i realized what i had done and Master just said to me, "Fuck boi, go to it! That's my Nazi slave!"

i was not being easy, my boxing was paying off as i hit him repeatedly, over and over, watching his face begin to swell. i liked the power that was emitting from my fists, my boots. It showed that while they looked powerful when i wore them, they were even more powerful when i used them. The guy was turning red in the face from the cord around his neck, he could barely stand. i looked down at my boots and could see they had lost their shine beneath the dirt and blood from this punk. i tore the cord and pushed his face onto my boots.

"Fucking clean them ass wipe," he didn't move so i slammed my other boot on the back of his neck. i could feel his teeth strike the leather and slowly he pushed his tongue out and started licking. My Master came around and ground his boot in the guy's ass, twisting and turning his lugs into the guy's skin. Master reminded the punk that we were going to show him full power tonight. Full power of Reich dick. The punk went to lift his head and i just pushed my boot harder into his neck. "Who told you to stop, those boots are still dirty."

"That's it boi, no mercy. You're serving the Reich and me, show him our power!"

The guy licked and licked as Master found more cord and started wrapping it around the guy's legs. He then took his knife and cut out a whole in his jeans revealing his white ass in briefs. Those didn't last long either. The bare butt was now visible. Master took his boot and left a nice boot print on his ass, then ground the dirt in deeper as he stuck his toe down the crack.

"boi, time to show him the full power," Master then grabbed me and kissed me so fucking hard, as the guy continued to lick my boot as my other boot ground into his head. my dick was growing now as Master raped my mouth. His hand grabbed my shirt and pulled me closer to him. i could feel the punk try to look at us under my boot. i let him, he needed to see these two skinheads kiss over him. That we were more powerful than him, he was the one lying in the garbage. i kneeled down to chew on Masters crotch and he pushed my head stronger into his BDU's. The punk was no longer under my boots, but he was continuing to lick them. i could feel Master's cock grow under his gray camo's, his leather gloved hands rubbing my shaved head. One hand reached down and was working my cock out from my bleached denim. i had to piss, even though i was getting hard. i let the flow go all over the punk. i could see the steam rise from him and smell the foul odor. The punk swore and i moved to aim the piss over his head.

Master never released the grip of my dick, working it harder as i had finished pissing. He brought his glove to my lips and i cleaned off the splatter of piss that remained. He shoved his thumb in deeper and i sucked on it. Master looked down at the punk, "he's my slave, and he is going to fuck your ass. he's never fucked anyone, but you're the first sign of life lower than my boi here." Master kicked his ass hard.

Master moved me around to behind the boi, as Master lowered and sat on the boi, facing me. i moved into position with my hard dick making a bulls eye for the target, this ripe punk ass. As i touched his ass cheek the punk started to yell and plead for us to stop. Master found some old rags and stuffed them in the kids mouth, then grabbed some plastic wrap and started wrapping it around the kid's face. i was getting fucking hard cause i wish that punk was me. i moved in and looked at Master. With no sound his lips said, "Fuck him boi!!"

i slammed my dick in dry and we heard the punk scream in the filthy rags. The plastic around his face was fogging up as he was having a harder time to breath. Master was right that i had never fucked anyone. The warmth of the fucker's ass was surrounding my dick. my body just knew how to fuck, it was so natural for me to dominate this guy. Over and over i pounded him. Master grabbed me by the neck and brought his lips to mine. His tongue filled my mouth, as my dick filled the punks ass. That shit head was covered with my skin boi piss, a slave raping his ass. He was learning that the Reich was power; we don't mess with anyone that messes with us.

Master reached around and pulled the plastic tighter around the punks face, cutting off his air. Master dug out his dick from his BDU's and i bent down to take it in. He was rock hard as he started to fuck his slave's face. i would feel the punk struggle under me. Moaning and screaming in the rags as his air was running out. i was reaching my climax, as was Master. Grabbing my head in his gloves, he slammed his Master cock down my throat shooting his load. Shortly i filled the punk's ass with my Nazi slave juice. Master held the plastic tight for a few more seconds, as the kid passed out.

Master pulled me up to his face, smiled like he never had and kissed me deeply and with more passion that ever. i pulled out and wiped my dick down with the punks shirt. We stood and pushed the passed out punk further in the trash. i fucking beat up the guy, i was high and my dick was rock hard. Master has taken me beyond my own abilities. i was his slave, but i was not to be abused by those outside the Reich. Master turned and dumped his piss on the still body. i bent down and licked off Masters boots. He patted me on the head. He pulled me up and we headed back to the room.

i could feel my dick growing in my pants, but i was fucking helpless with this straight jacket on. i rolled over on my stomach and started to grind it in the padded floor. That is when i heard the steel door open. i heard them laughing as a boot pushed my ass into the mat. "Fucking faggot," was all i heard.

i must have fallen asleep. When i woke my face was covered with sweat. The isolation room was hotter than hell. The smell of the leather straightjacket was filling the space, as was my boots. Since i went out, i have no idea how long i have been in here. Hunger was starting to set in. With the sweat rolling down my face, the tape around my head was slowly coming loose as i worked my jaw. It would be a while before i get it off, but it will happen.

i rolled off my stomach to find my BDU's stuck to the plastic of the room padding. It came back to me now. They had come into the room to find me grinding my dick into the padding. i was thinking back to when Sir had me fuck that asshole in Atlanta. That got me so fucking hard. Thinking about that guy with his hands tied in the garbage, Master holding that plastic bag over his head. Fuck what control! Then he had me fuck him, as he fucked my face. Fuck, my dick is growing again just thinking of this. Feeling the stiff material against it. The cops must have been watching on close circuit TV. Since i had my face in the mat, i never saw them. One of them pushed his boot right into my ass, grinding my crotch deeper in the mat.

The smell of the leather was filling me, as was the bondage i was in. Gagged and helpless under the boots of these fucking cop who have no right to keep me here! One of them was yelling at the top of his lungs at me, calling me shit, and faggot. Big fucking deal, like i don't know i'm a faggot. i knew cops weren't smart, but were they really that dumb?!

Then i felt something cold on the back of my neck and the distinct click. The weapon pressed further into my neck. Right next to my ear i felt a warm breath. Then a whisper.

"Fucking blow your load for us boi."

The boot that was grinding me, kicked me between my legs striking my balls. i yelled into the gag. The gun slammed my head back on the mat.

"Come on faggot, blow that load!"

Another kick to the balls. my head was held firmly by the weapon, as the warm breath crossed my cheek and ears. my shaved head felt it all, as the sweat ran off the top, down my face and into my eyes.

The boot crashed into my balls again, as my ass was struck with a hard thin object. It has to be one of their batons. It struck again and again. Harder and harder. This was more relentless than the boot kicking my balls. The guy with the weapon kept it grinding in my neck and i humped the pad trying to shoot my load for these guys entertainment.

my breath was cut off by the plastic covering my face. They were pulling a plastic bag over my head. i heard duct tape coming off the role and it was wrapped about my neck. The plastic was pulled in with every breath in. The gun struck the side of my face, as the baton came down on my ass and the boot kicked.

"Fucking do it boi!"

Sweat was covering my plastic covered face, breathing was getting hard. i couldn't get the sock out of my mouth, so i could only breath through my nose. The plastic would cover my nostrils, i would gasp for air. Another kick to the nuts, as the gun held my face down. i continued humping, as my breath was running out. i tried to arch my back, but i couldn't for they wouldn't let my head up. my eyes were fading, i was passing out. One last kick to the balls as the baton worked its way through my BDU's into my asshole. i felt my balls warm then the cum shoot from the hole into my BDU's. my breathing races, as i was blacking out. Through the bag i heard, "You might think about who you're fucking with in the alley next time faggot."

The last load of cum shot out as i realize, they knew something about the attack i did on the guy in Atlanta. i groaned loudly and faded out.

Now it was all clear, they had picked me up because they knew i was the one that fucked that guy. How did they find out? Or was one of them the guy? Shit, i could really be screwed. i need to piss something awful, so i just let it. They couldn't do much more to me at this point. my ass hurt like hell, as did my balls. i was here for a while, it would be until Master returned from Chicago before he would miss me and begin looking for me.

The room filled with light and i shut my eyes. There before me stood the cop that brought me in. He smiled then spit on me. His look changed, "You piss in our cell?"

He grabbed my feet and dragged me out. Kicking me a few times, he rolled me on my stomach and started undoing the straightjacket. He rolled me over where i found his weapon pointing straight in my face.

"Don't get any ideas as I take you out of this. I'm moving you. Play it cool and you'll not be hurt again."

i had had enough in the room, i didn't feel like fighting at this point. And it would be stupid anyway. How many other cops were outside the door? After getting me out of the jacket, he stood me up and walked me to the other side of the room. Sitting me down in a plastic chair with what looked like seat belts on it. He secured my wrists down at my side with some Velcro straps that buckled, then my ankles around my boots. Then he started with the seatbelt like straps and locked me into this seat. i was not able to move.

When he was done he stood back, looking at me with a slight wicked grin. He walked away, out the door. i looked around for the first time to see i was alone in this room with this chair. There was nothing else. The coolness of the air conditioning was wonderful. i just relaxed, stretching my muscles as best as i could.

i heard some laughter on the other side of the door, then it opened and the cop returned. He wasn't laughing when he entered. He stood before me, staring me down. i had learned how to stare with my training with Sir, so he wouldn't win this game. Of course, i didn't expect him to reach out and grab my bottom lip pinching it and twisting it. Fuck, it hurt like a bitch! He was showing me that he had control of me.

Drawing out his night stick, he brought it before me. Slowly he rubbed it gently around my face, neck, throat and head. It was almost sensual. Around and around the coolness of the painted wood slid across my drying skin. i continued to keep his eyes in mine. Never letting him think he had me. The stick came up to my lips and slowly made their way into them. Was this the guy i had fucked in the alley? He was being pretty easy with me, almost like he wanted to have sex with me. But i doubt that would happen.

He removed the stick from my lips and lightly moved it around my body. He toyed with the buttons on my Fred Perry shirt, passing over my tits. Moving slowly, circling my pecs, then down my abs to my crotch. He slid the stick over my crotch, just enough for me to twitch. But i never let me eyes leave his. He pressed the stick under my crotch making me lift my ass off the seat. He quickly pulled out the stick and struck it in his other hand rather sharply. The smack of it striking his leather glove broke the silence in the room. Then he slowly brought it back to my lips. Holding my head he forced open my lips and worked the night stick in my mouth and down my throat. Further and further he pushed, until i almost gagged.

As if he wanted me to give a blow job to the stick, he moved it up and down. He gently took my lips and moved them closed around the stick. In and out, as the stick was lubed with my saliva. i could feel my dick growing again. What was it about this cop that was keeping me hard! He removed the stick and let me lick the shaft of it. Coating it over and over, making it a wet shine. Then the stick went into my mouth. my head was forced back as he pushed it further in. At that point i lost eye contact with him. i heard a slight grunt of humor as he noticed this.

This went on for a while. Then he let go of the stick while it was deep in my throat. He told me not to let it fall out, so i had to keep my head up. i heard the jangle of some keys and the zipper on his uniform shirt. He took the stick in his hands again and lowered my head. There before me was the chest of an Adonis. It was well defined, strong and showed power. His leather gloved hand stroked his chest, and then grabbed a tit tightly, pulling on it. He moaned. i wanted to lick that chest. He took the stick and put it down his pants, working his crotch with it behind his uniform pants. Stirring in my bondage, i wanted to get my dick out of the hard patch of material it was trapped behind. my breathing was increasing as i wanted to touch this Man. He brought the stick out of his pants and put it back in my mouth. i could taste the cop sweat on the stick, mixing with my spit. He spun the stick around in my mouth. Twisting it and lowering it as far as it would go. Letting go of it again, i heard the leather of his belt squeak and it drop to the floor. When he let me lower my head, he was naked before me, his breaches around his boots. He slowly pulled the stick out of my mouth with a pop at the end. Working the stick around his chest, down his abs to his crotch then around to his ass. i couldn't believe what happened next as he started to insert the stick in his ass. This fucking pig was killing me here.

He worked the stick in his ass, breathing heavy and staring at me with a wicked grin on his lips. As the stick worked it, i was snapped from my horny state by his other gloved hand strongly slapping my face. He spit on my face, slapping me hard and harder. The gloved hand hit me on the backhand and the forehand. He spit over and over, one time hitting my tongue as my mouth was open with pain. i glanced between his legs to see him working feverishly with the stick. He struck me again and again. Between a hit, he pushed towards me and shoved his dick in my lips. my dick grew instantly as that pig cop's dick filled my mouth. His grew also, choking me. He continued to slap me and i could feel him spitting on my shaved head. i could see nothing but his crotch hairs and smell the stale piss from earlier in the day. Then everything stopped as he stiffened and my throat could feel the slickness of his cum shooting from this cops dick. His leather gloved hand grabbed the back of my head as he forced himself deeper in my throat.

He collapsed holding me tightly. i am not sure, but i think i felt a slight kiss on my head. As he pulled out his dick i cleaned it off. Just as his dick head left my lips, the night stick filled my lips. i could taste to cops shit as he twisted the stick around my tongue. i cleaned it also. He took care of his clothing, getting back in full uniform. Returned the night stick to its holder and he left the room.

my dick was bursting to release, but i couldn't for i was helpless in this chair. Struggling with the belts, it was useless. i growled loudly, but knew they wouldn't come to release me.

The pains in my stomach were intense; it had been hours perhaps days since i had eaten. Being alone in a room with no windows doesn't give me any idea as to the time. The boi's dick has since shriveled, but thoughts of the encounter with the cop's night stick brought it to life on occasion. Eventually the door opened and the cop that fucked me returned. Without emotion, he came to me and started undoing the restraints.

"You're being moved. Come to find out, you're pretty hot property."

i decide to keep my mouth shut and see where this is all leading. After he releases everything but my wrists, he reaches under the seat and pulls out a leather hood. Roughly putting it on me, he laces it up and locks the collar around my neck. He then puts on a thick gag that is also locked on. Last, he snaps on a blindfold. Releasing my hands, he has me stand and puts handcuffs on me with my hands behind my back.

Finally i am allowed to leave the room as i am marched out the door, with the cops hand on my shoulder. Where i go, i am not sure, but soon i am being forced in the back of what must be a van. A tarp or something is thrown over me and i hear the doors close.

With the leather surrounding my head, it is hard to hear anything but my breathing. i hear a few voices outside the van. The sound of doors opening and closing, then the vibration of the van's engine. As the vehicle pulls out, i slide back, my feet hitting the wall or door.

They drive for a long while then stop, as i hear one say they need gas. i think there is more than one of them as two doors open and close. Through the drive they have been very quiet, except for a few words about the Reich and our mission. i hear them talking outside the van and try to control my breathing to listen to what they are saying.

"….has been so fucking easy!"

"Don't get excited yet. We gonna bring down that guy. He knows we got his boi, so now he will pay attention," my interest increase in this conversation.

"You sure you want to follow through with this, it could be our asses."

"Once he we finish him off, his Master will want revenge and we got him!"

my breathing stops as i take in the full implications of what they just said. They are going to snuff me out! my heart stops and i start struggling in my bondage. i need to get out of here. Gently i feel around with my boots and think i feel the door and the latch a ways up on the wall that my feet are against. But where are we and how will i get out. Just then the doors slam and the van is moving again. i play it cool for now as i don't want them to know that i know what is going on.

The smooth road turns rough as i think they have turned onto a forest road. As they travel the bumps toss me around the back of the van. Then i hear one of them yell, "Get out of the fucking way!" They are pissed as the van comes to a stop. I make out part of the conversation as i hear another voice. Seems like a 4x4 truck is stuck in the middle of the road and they are asking these guys for help. i hear the doors slam as one of them is swearing up a storm.

I move my feet around again and eventually find the latch to the door. i press on it and with the grip of my lug soles on my Rangers, i am able to pull it down. i hear a small latch release and feel the door move away from my foot. Unable to see because of the fucking leather hood, i move around to get out from under the tarp. i try my hands, but they are securely locked in the cuffs. Moving slowly, i am able to make my way towards the opening of the van. First my feet, then legs get out, bending at the knees if feel the dirt below me. i work slowly and get myself up right.

i am out of the van, but i can't see one fucking thing. Barely, i can smell the dirt and the trees. Very slowly i start to step away. But i don't want to them to find me gone. So i step back and gently shut the door until it latches. i can hear the voices as they are working on the 4x4, so i try to move in the other direction, i hope. The ground is a bit soft, like it has been raining as i work my way out into the woods, with no gawd damn sight.

i must have taken some 100 steps when i trip and land face first in a pit of mud and water. i pull myself out and catch my breath. i feel the water soaking my Fred Perry and BDU's, as i roll around and discover there is a large log next to me. i roll on my side and feel with my hands an opening under the log. Working as best as i can, i push myself in under the log and hope that they don't notice i am gone.

my breathing relaxes as i get settled. i am totally screwed if i can't get the blindfold off, but i am going to wait until i know they are gone. A loud roar of an engine fills the woods as i think they 4x4 is started. There is a burst of cheers and the sounds of doors, opening and another vehicle started. Lying very still i listen as it seems they drive off and all is silent.

Figuring the log is rough; i start rubbing my head against the bark hoping that it might catch the blindfold and unsnap it. The cuffs are cutting into my wrists and i am getting cold in my wet uniform. Over and over i rub, almost making the leather warm in patches, when i hear the first snap come undone. So i press harder with my head and the open piece of the blindfold against the bark. Turning slowly, i get another one to unsnap then another. Crushing my nose, i get two more and then the blindfold falls away.

Working my way out from under the log, i find that it is nearly dark. Lost in the woods at night, cuffed and gagged. Great! What would Sir do? Starting to walk it wasn't long until if found the dirt road. But i figured i would not take that since they might return. So i paced out a distance from the road and turned. Then i heard the engine and the slivers of light that came around the trees. Lowering behind a stump, i saw a white van with the sheriff's logo on the door. They were back. Since they hadn't parked, i started running. Then i heard the gun shot! Tripping i crashed into a tree. i worked myself up and started running again. my breathing was difficult with the fucking gag in my mouth and i started to sweat in the hood. i couldn't run fast but i kept a good pace. Another shot and it hit the tree not far from me. As i turned around to look behind me i saw a flashlight. The ground disappeared beneath my feet and i tumbled down a wooded incline to find myself landing on a fallen tree, knocking the wind out of me as my chest hit.

i could barely keep up with my breathing through my nose and i heard one of them up the hill yelling at me to stay still. Another shot was fired as i lifted my head, but it hit near me, the splinters hitting my arms. A hand grabbed my head and slammed me into the tree, i felt warm liquid around my nose, figuring it was bleeding.

"I got the fucker! Over here!" he yelled to his partner.

"Coming!"

"You fucker, you think you can escaped hooded and cuffed like that? You are too stupid to live!"

i feel the gun against my neck. "You fucking faggots have ruined this country. Well, you're gonna start the end of Faggotville."

i felt the back of my BDU's rip, as he kept the gun to my neck. Then he moved it down my back towards my ass. He pushed the gun at my hole and worked it in. He started to dry fuck me with his weapon. "This, boy, is gonna be your final fuck that will blow your ass off," he laughs as he shoves it in deep and painfully.

i yell in the gag, i hate to admit it but i let my Master down. i was begging for mercy, for them to let me go. But he continued to fuck me with his weapon; i think he wanted his buddy to be there when he blew my ass. i don't want to admit it Sir, but i started to cry. It hurt so much and i was so afraid. This was beyond anything that you and i had done. i always knew i was safe with you Sir. But now i was alone and in the hands of these freaking asshole cops.

i felt something warm on my leg and i knew the cop was pissing on me as he was gun fucking me. Then i felt the piss move quickly up my leg on my back and away. The gun was left stuck in my ass but no force on it. There was struggling, grunting, but i didn't dare turn around. Then i heard it, the sound i've heard before and knew well. It was the sound of a pair of Rangers hitting a guy's skull. Not to kill someone, but knock them out. i turned and my eyes swelled with tears. It was you Sir!! You were there in the wood saving your boi, your Nazi slave boi!

Over and over you kicked the fucking cop, soiling his uniform until he didn't move. You turned to me and that smile that i have fallen in love with came across your face. Slowly you worked your way to me. Your gloved hand stroked my hooded head and you grabbed me and kissed me through the locked gag. i broke down in tears. Sobbing like a baby as you held me tight. The gun dropped out of my ass. You laid me gently on the log again while opening your uniform pants. There in the woods, my Nazi Master in his black uniform fucked me with no mercy. i sobbed, soaking the leather hood with my tears, but i was so hard, so glad to be feeling you Sir in me. i didn't think that i would ever again. Your gloved hand came across my head and squeeze my nose shut cutting off my air as you shot your load in my ass. Reclaiming your boi. You lowered me down off the log and we sat, you holding me so tight and i cried the final tears of joy.

"boi, not sure how you got this way, but you'll have to wait till we get home to get you out."

i nodded yes.

"I think I might have to keep you locked up in a cage from now on when I leave. Guess you are too popular of a prize," he said with a smile. i lowered my head on his chest and he hugged me tightly.

"I love you boi, don't ever forget that."

i was so weak i nearly started crying again. You held me and told me it was ok to cry, that boi's are weak and they cry for their

Masters. For when one serves as well as i do, there is no way i can live without you Sir.

Slowly, you stood up and i saw in the moonlight of the woods, my Master in his black BDU's, bomber jacket with arm band and his Dehner's. i worked myself around, kneeling before you and kissed your boots through my gag.

Someday Sir, i know you'll let me out of this cage for the danger will pass. But for now i can remember the good times that we had. You teach me not to be afraid, but in this cage i can't show you how strong i am. You faced the enemy and won. i will do the same.

Meeting Skin

You can feel the evil in them, just with one glance. The shaved head, heavy boots used to kick the shit out of those that have crossed them, the sneer that intimates those around them. And damn, if all that and more makes me crave to kneel before them and lick their white laced boots.

While it is deeply hidden, service to the skins is something I have craved for a while now. Living here in London has allowed me to see skins almost on a daily basis. I never really knew how far my submissive streak went until I finally came face to face with one skin.

I had seen him in the area, many times. While I would never venture out in the skin kit that I had worked up, I would wear it at night, think of him as I wanked in a black hanky just like the one he wore in his back pocket. In my dreams, he would take me to his flat, bind me up and flog the shit out of me. Make me drink is Guinness laced piss, then kick the shit out of me before leaving me gagged with his dirty jock for the night after fucking me so deep I swore I would sing in the boy's choir next Boxing Day. While doing this dreaming I found I was surfing the web checking out the skinhead sites and traveling darker into the neo Nazi gay skins. At first I thought them silly, but damn if this deeper evil just made my lust to serve grow. I knew I had to serve one skin, be educated to serve him best and my life would be set on a path I could not return from.

Waking one morning, I needed my morning Starbucks. Not thinking, I pulled on a shirt and headed down to the local spot. As I was almost half way there, the clunk of my boots brought me to reality that I was outside in my skin kit. My 14 holes had white laces, my bleachers where tight with braces and I even had grabbed my FP shirt. Fuck if I didn't start to sweat. What if someone I knew saw me in this get up? And if a skin or two… they'd laugh their asses off, cause of my blond hair. Never had I had the courage to actually shave my head. But I was more than half way to the "Bucks" so I just continued.

Ordering went without incident, and I was starting to get a little randy in my kit. I think one or two of the neighboring fags were checking me out. Hell, if a skin makes me rock hard, what was I doing to them? Heading to the door, I was checking one of those pervs out. He wasn't half bad looking, wearing a rugby shirt from some team up north. But any thoughts of anything with him were shattered when I crashed in a brick wall. His name was Trevor, complete with the black hanky in his back pocket. My drink spilled from the cup and splattered on Trevor's camos and boots. The rest of the coffee was grabbed from my hand, my neck grabbed tightly and I was being forced to his boots.

"Lick 'em cunt!"

I couldn't believe, here in the doorway of a Starbucks, I was about to touch the leather of his boots with my tongue. I didn't hesitate, I just did it. The mixture of leather and mocha was actually good and I licked deeply. As I was finishing up, I felt his leather belt go around my neck and tightened. I was dragged from the Starbucks, as a few watched but really didn't do anything. Perhaps since we were both dressed like skin's they didn't worry. Because no one gets involved with skins.

I barely kept up with his pace, as the belt was chocking me. Through the busy street he led me, until we reached an alley and he shoved me back against the wall.

His arm rested snuggly against my throat, cutting off my air. As I looked up, there was his eyes, blue, staring me down. He was not showing any bit of remorse in what he had or was going to do to me. His nose twitched in a slight tense, and then he moved closer and slammed his lips against mine. My knees almost gave out from under me, as his tongue carved my lips open and explored deep inside. As he kissed me, he poured the hot remaining coffee down my pants and I moaned into his lips. As he pulled back, his teeth took my bottom lip and pinched them to the point of nearly breaking the skin. He let go and I took in my breath.

"I knew you were a skin at heart. You been checking me out and you just had to taste my boots."

Fuck, had he known about my lust for him the entire time.

"Be here tonight at 10, and I'll show you what being skin is."

He spit on my face, leaned forward and licked it off and took off. Just like that, he was gone. And my burning dick was glowing with excitement. It was all I could do just to not start wanking right there!

Walking home, people must have thought I was some basket case that pissed his pants, but I didn't fucking care. Even with the leather belt hanging from around my neck, I just didn't give a fuck. Tonight I was going to be with a skin. The hottest fucking skin there is. I didn't care about fear, I want to serve.

I was gonna clean my kit that day before meeting up with Trevor that night. But I remembered what I had learned online about skins and liking things dirty. After all, before he left, Trev spit on my face and cleaned it so quickly. So I didn't even change that day. I actually had some reports to write and spent the day working on them, in communication with my business partner. He would have laughed knowing what I was wearing. While we've worked together for 5 years, he still doesn't know my fetish for skins. It's just as well, for I'm not sure how he'd react. Hell, I know he'd be pissed that I was going out here in 5 minutes to meet this oxen of a man. I know I am going to end up regretting locking the door behind me tonight. But this one of those things that you do, not because of your brain but because of the raw lust in your crotch.

Fucking cold and wet, typical night in London. Standing, waiting to taste those boots again. Oh and that raping of my mouth was beyond obscene. Damn, if I didn't want more. I was glad I wore my MA1, it helped keep some of the drizzle off, but even that was starting to soak in. I heard a noise to my right, turning I found this skin that I lusted after coming towards me. At first the bright alley lights behind him only made him a silhouette. It was like out of one of those stupid Hollywood action flicks. But I eventually could see him more and I think I might have grunted. He had turned in his BDU's to have tight leather pants on, tucked into the 20 hole Rangers. His MA1 actually had an arm band on the right arm and he carried a baseball bat. This really scared me, for I began to worry that my lust might have hooked me up with a skin that is not gay. Some of those straight skins could be ruthless when I comes to being a faggot. But I worried less as he got near me and smiled. I was staring deep into his blue eyes and didn't even see the bat strike my side and bring me crashing to the dirty wet cobblestone.

"Fucking cunt, you really want to serve don't you?"

I couldn't get a word out, cause my lungs were trying to get air in from being sideswiped. Just then his boot came up and caught my chin and flew my back into a pile of garbage bags. As my lungs filled again, the stench was horrible. I couldn't tell if it was drizzle or blood but something was running down my chin. As he grabbed the collar of my jacket, now was the time for me to leave. This was beyond anything I'd ever wanked too and was convinced that I would be dead in an alley very shortly.

But no words came out of my mouth. He dragged me across the cobblestone until I was able to get to my feet. He slammed me against the wall, with my cheek kissing the brick. Pressing against me, I felt his hand run down my ass and under my crotch squeezing tightly my balls. I opened my mouth to yell, and he shoved a wet cloth in. It was followed by a leather type gag that pressed the cloth in deeper.

"I pissed on that before I came, so it is nice and moist for you." he whispered in my ear. As I swallowed I took in the salty taste for the first time. He pulled a wool ski mask over me, to cover up the gag, he quickly cuffed my hands behind my back. He pulled me away and we headed out of the alley.

The interior of his large flat was quite different from the exterior. Inside the touches of a decorator were of a classic European flair. While I was raced through the rooms, I was able to catch glimpses of pieces from the war. Some pieces looked to be very rare and could be expensive. I wondered just what Trevor did to afford such things. Coming down the stairs to the basement, I nearly fell as he left little time for me to hit each step with my booted foot. I was getting cold from the soaked hood on my head, and the water drenching my coat, shirt and jeans.

Taking me to the center of the room, near the coal furnace, he put me on my knees. Removing his jacket to show a white tank shirt with the eagle crest on the chest he turned and stared me down. He walked around me; I could feel the stare cut my skin, shave my head and rape my ass. I wanted to look up at him, but I only peeked at his boots as they passed in front of me. He stopped with his bulging leather crotch in my face. It was so close I could smell the wet leather, but I didn't dare to touch it with my lips.

"You're here cause you want to be here."

Was that a question or an observation? I couldn't tell and I couldn't respond with this pissed rag in my throat.

"You have no choice, what is going to happen is going to happen."

And it did. Before I knew it, I was mummified head to toe in rubber, then tape. He had removed only the gag to stick some sort of gag that kept my mouth open. I couldn't see the outside world; I was alone in this tape cocoon. Through it all, he never spoke, he was distance as if wanting me to beg to do something, but I didn't know what I could beg for. Hell, I was owned by him now. I was helpless from the time he forced me to lick the coffee from his boots. He knew it and was going to show me things I only dreamed at night.

I was laid down and further secured. My hearing was muffled by plugs that he had placed in my ears. After laying me down, an urge of pleasure came over me when he must have started to take my dick into his mouth. I'd been blown by the best of them, but this guy was the Master. Totally helpless, I could only struggle in the bondage I was in, as he worked me closer and closer to orgasm. My only connection to breath was through a hose he had connected to the open gag and that was now closed. Now I was truly helpless, was he going to off me now? I arched my back trying to get to that final stage and shoot my load. I knew he wanted it, for then he would own me totally. As my breathing faded, I felt something in the tube and it filled my mouth. Fuck, something was being poured down the tube. It tasted like a beer and it wasn't stopping. This was more difficult for I had to breathe and drink, while he was taking me beyond the stars. I was gonna get drunk with all this beer and he knew it. But I was drunk with lust, I was pumping his face with my dick and he took it all the way down. Deeper and deeper he let me go. My fists were in balls taped so tight, I could hardly move them, my wet clothes covered me, under a layer of rubber and tape, trapped in my boots, jeans, MA1, gagged and being sucked by the hottest fucking skin that walked the planet. I was going to serve him forever, I had no doubt. Sir, this slave is yours.

He let go of my dick as the cum burst forth, landing in the tube that lead to my mouth. I must have pumped a great deal, for it slowly filled my mouth, mixing with the beer I had downed.

I've never been sure how long I was in that bondage. He left me that way for days, working my mind and training me to serve him. To reinforce a point, he would bring me to ecstasy over and over. At times, I would nearly pass out for the intensity of the sessions. While I rested, he fed me more beer and piss. He was ruthless in his punishment of me in this helpless state. At times he would cut away parts of the tape and rubber and use his stun gun on me. Voltage would make me want to burst from the cocoon, but I was helpless and my screams were muffled by a filthy rag he would stuff in the tube in my mouth. I know I pissed on and in myself, for he would run the hose from my dick to my mouth. I would feel his boots over and over all over my body. And when I was ready to beg for release, he would start again with me sexually. He was hitting each button that made my dick grow, in his mouth, in his hand, in his ass. He let me rest and listen to tapes he had made about submission, serving him and his ideals, how I wanted nothing more in life than what I had now and when I left I would miss him and be helpless without him. Just listening to these tapes, in his voice, would bring me to the edge over and over again. Often I would fall sleep listening to his voice. I was so safe where I was, I didn't want to leave.

That was all a few months ago. I am his slave, through and through. I have done a great deal of learning on my own and with his guidance. I have sunk into a neo Nazi gay skin world that I never dreamed I would have actually live a life. I've met a few of his mates, but he never allows them to touch me. He is very protective of me, but tells me that someday I will become a true skin. I've come so far, and I know I will make him proud in doing so.

I'm half wasted as I write this, because he and I were out at the pub after a ride on his ZX-1. He wears his full leathers, while I am only allowed my skin kit. But I wear it with pride now, because I understand the loyalty and honour it is to be allowed to wear it while serving Trevor. Its amazing to me that I'm almost there, I'm almost a true skin.

The Birthday

Trey and I have been friends for quite a while now, we've played a few times, but mostly we've developed a great friendship. We were going to the movies today, the first time we've hooked up in a couple of weeks. When I arrived at his apartment, he was fiddling on his computer. I made myself comfortable on the sofa as he finished up his stuff. We had plenty of time before the movie started. After he finished, he came and sat in the chair next to the sofa. We talked about what we both had been up too in the last couple of weeks. While we talk on line a lot, we still always have something to talk about in person. Trey looked pretty hot in his 14 hole black boots and matching black t-shirt with bold white letters spelling out "Skinhead". There was a shine to his shaved head reflecting the sun coming through the blinds of his small apartment.

We were talking and laughing like guys do when I found my hand touching his shoulder. It was just a brief touch, but it sure felt good to touch him, again. He must have liked it, because he gently brushed me on the arm. Then it started the touching and slight tickling. He knows my sensitive spots. Our booted feet were playing with each other, hands on the legs, stroking.

Before long, he had my Ben Sherman shirt undone and his hands were tweaking at my tits. He was saying how they should be pierced because that would give him something to work with. I shuttered a little bit, not liking the thought of the needle going through my tits. I worked my shirt off and felt his hands against my skin. They were warm and rough from the construction work he does. He has shown me, rather intimately, the leather gloves he wears for work, but his hands were still rough. I worked my hands around his body and we took each other in a warm tender hug.

He ran his hands along my snug denim covered legs, as I lifted my booted foot and played with his crotch through his jeans. He smiled at me, knowing that I was playing a dirty little trick. He stood, going to a drawer and pulled out some white rope. I suddenly felt that the movies were not going to happen tonight. I stood and he came to me, putting my hands behind me and laced them up, nice and snug. He reached in another drawer and brought out his leather cop gloves. Putting them on he ran his hands over by body, they felt so comforting. He brought one hand up to my face and let me take in the fine leather scent, as his other hand pinched my tit rather hard. My pain was muffled by this hand as he gagged me tightly.

"I think you need some training." Trey whispered in my ear.

That made my cock grow in my Under Armor jock. Feeling the smooth of the UA against my cock, mixing with my pre-cum, I just moaned into his gloved hand.

He led me to the bed where I sat. He worked my belt loose, followed by my zipper and unbuttoned my jeans. He was feeling inside my pants, and worked around inside my jock. If I would've known, I wouldn't have worn them. Trey unlaced my boots, and slipped them off, then pulling off my socks. He took my toes into his mouth and sucked and licked them. Fuck!! I was squirming, if felt so fucking good. He then stood and pulled my jeans off, quickly followed by my jock. I was now naked, with my wrists tied behind my back. Man, it had been along time since I was in this position, it felt wonderful. He had me work myself on the bed, where he tied my ankles together and then laced them to the foot board of the bed. He had me sit up and undid my wrists. He then bound my wrists in front of me. Then, he took them and moved them above my head tying them to the headboard. He rubbed his gloved hands all over my body, playing with my sensitive areas. I giggled, yipped, and moaned as his hands played my body. I wasn't going anyplace, but I struggled against the ropes. I love the feeling of helplessness that I have bound like this. He stepped away for a moment and returned with a ball gag. He installed it and I was now a bit quieter as he worked my body again. My under arms, my sides, my bellybutton. It was getting more sensitive as time passed.

He stepped away again and returned with a small black plastic bag. This worried me as he began to put it over my head. But once he had it on me, I found my nose was placed in a hole in the bag. It was somewhat dark, but I could see faint shadows. Then I heard the sound of a roll of tape being undone. A strip of wide, most likely duct tape, was placed over my eyes. I was in the dark now. Trey continued to tape my entire head into the bag. It was tight; yet, my skin wasn't being pulled by the tape. The tape covered my mouth, and neck down to the bottom of the bag. Trey then put on a leather collar on my neck. I couldn't see, nor speak, and could only barely hear. The assault began, as I knew my nose was clear and I was safe in all respects. My tits were twisted at times, Trey played with my balls and rubbed the pre-cum on my dick just for teasing. He reached under me and fingered my ass. He tickled the bottoms of my feet. I could only bounce around on the bed, moaning, and totally enjoying that lack of any control over my situation.

Things were going very nicely, I had forgotten about time and was unsure how long I'd been in this state, when the telephone rang. He talked for less than a moment and hung up. He told me it was a wrong number. He started the assault on my naked, bound body again. He produced ice cubes and melted them on my warm body. He was playing with my dick when I noticed there were another set of hands touching me. This set of hands was not wearing gloves. They were soft hands, a bit cold to the touch but warming quickly against my body. I panicked slightly, not knowing what the hell was happening. But the four hands really started the work. They were tickling my sensitive spots, fingering my ass, squeezing my balls, rubbing my dick, twisting my tits and occasionally plugging my nose. Then Trey asked if I was alright, and I responded in a grunt and nodding head that I was doing fine. I trusted Trey and knew that who ever was also playing with me would not hurt me.

After being questioned by Trey, rope was tied around my cock and balls. It was tight and felt wonderful. My balls were stretched and tied to my big toes. My dick must have been sticking straight up with the rope jacket now on it. The ice cubes returned and I began to struggle against ropes, but my balls were being pulled at the same time. Then someone took a hold of my dick head and started to rub. I couldn't stay still, another hand was twisting my tits as another worked at playing with my ass, just barely entering enough for a tease. I was crazy with excitement, ecstasy, and my body was enjoying every second. They continued for the longest time, or what seemed like the longest time.

Then they stopped, and I moaned into the gag. They let me know that I wasn't done with. They flipped me over onto my stomach, positioning my head on the side so I could still breathe. There was a tug on my bound balls, but the way Trey had bound me, I was easily turned over without having to undo any of the ropes. My roped hard dick was smashed into the mattress. Then my ass was slapped by a hand. I was surprised, as it tugged on my balls. The slaps continued, not hard, just enough to know that I was not going to be leaving this position and I would have to take what ever was being dished out. Hands began running up and down my back, sometimes with fingernails. My feet were played with, which in turn tugged on my balls. Then a finger returned to my ass, as ice cubes were melted down my ass crack. Then the lubed finger slightly entered my ass, and it moved around, playing. The other hands continued their assault, as my ass hole was teased. Then all was stopped, and I could feel them leave the room. I lay on the bed, feeling the ropes against my skin, the sweat pouring from my head wrapped in plastic, my balls boiling with wanted release.

I felt someone working on the ropes around my feet and ankles. My toes and thus, my balls, were released. My cock and balls were still tightly tied, but no longer stretched.

My hands were released from the headboard, but my wrists remanded tied. I was rolled over and my tied wrists were tied to the ropes around my cock and balls. They then wrapped my hands in tape so that I couldn't play with myself. I was stood up from the bed and made to walk. I couldn't see, but soon I felt the cold hard floor. I was being lead into the bathroom and helped into the tub. The four hands had me get down to my knees. And I heard their footsteps out of the bathroom. It tried to touch my dick with my taped hands but it wasn't much use with the rope wrapped about my dick. And as I moved my hands, I also tugged on my nuts. I heard the two return and then the sound of opening soda liter bottles. I soon felt liquid running down my head, and suddenly I felt cold soda running all over my skin. I could smell a cola; it was cold and made my body tingle and shiver. It was running all over me, and it didn't seem to stop. It was a strange sensation that I had never felt. It felt as if they each dumped four liters each on me, I was sticky and cold. Then I felt warmth on my skin, liquid warmth. Then the odor filled my nose, someone was urinating on me. It was warming, and tingling on my body. As one stopped, someone else started to cover the areas that were missed before. As the second one finished, I was instructed to stand. As I stood, the soda and urine dripped from my body. A unique odor had been created, I was sticky and pissy.

I shortly found my hands being untaped and my wrists released.

I was handed my jeans and instructed to put them on. I slid my snug fitting bleachers on my sticky skin and could feet the denim start to stick and soak up the fluids. My hard dick could hardly fit in my jeans, and when I zipped them up, I felt my cock and balls tightly bound inside. I was allowed to step out of the tub and onto a towel. My boots were handed to me and blindly I put them on, while sitting on the tub edge. I was made to stand again, and two mild tit clamps were attached to my tits. I was handed my shirt and I put it on. Then the tape was cut from my head and the plastic bag removed. I looked to find only Trey smiling at me. He reached around and removed the ball gag. When I went to speak, he put his hand over my mouth and told me not to speak.

He lead my out of the bathroom and who ever was there was now gone. Trey put cuffs on my wrists and laid my bomber jacket over them to cover them. Without a word, we headed out the door down the hall of his apartments and out the front door. As we stepped out on to the sidewalk, a van pulled up and the side door was opened, I was shoved in by Trey as he followed me in. Before I could really see what was in the van, my eyes were blindfolded with a bandanna and a leather dick gag shoved in my mouth. I was laid on the floor of the van with my feet spread eagled then my cuffs released and my arms spread eagled. Someone grabbed at my crotch and I moaned. Then I heard Trey's voice in my ear, "Happy Birthday .... We're going to your party!"

He laughed an evil laugh as the van continued down the road.

My clothes where sticking to my skin as I felt every bump and turn the van made. Occasionally, a hand reached over and played the my tits, or squeezed my tight crotch.

Time passed by, but I was unsure of how much. I could've been on the van floor for minutes or hours. And if I thought I could keep track of where in the city we might be, well, that just wasn't happening. After a bit, Trey was unbuttoning my shirt. He tied a string to the chain between the tit clamps, stretching my tits some. It wasn't extremely painful, but I wasn't moving much. He unzipped my jeans, fishing out my tied cock and balls. He tied my hard dick head snugly and stretched it straight up. If I was to move or we went over a bump, well there was a tug. Just about the time Trey was finished with stringing me up, the van came to a halt and the engine turned off. Without a word, I hear the two of them leave. The doors slammed shut. Now here I was pretty much alone in this strange van. My dick tied up, my tits stretched and there was no way I was going to get out of the binds. Still, a thought ran through my head. Does this van have windows? Are people walking by, getting a free show. And just how long was I going to be left alone in the van. And what if someone broke in and stole it, boy would they get more than they bargained for! I'd try to struggle to see if I might get loose, but then I'd be reminded of my stretched tits.

Then my mind wondered back to the events that lead up to this, I was staying pretty hard through all this. We had done something's that I never expected Trey to be interested in or he had been thinking of. I had been played with by a stranger and have yet to know who he is. I'm in a strange van, headed to who knows where to face who know what. But I was enjoying the lack of knowledge and control. And I knew that Trey would keep me safe. Plus I have the control of the safe word, the one that has not even crossed my mind. I was a bit apprehensive, look at my position, who wouldn't? But damn, this was one of the best experiences of my sexual life so far. What had Trey planned to top it?

My thoughts were broken by the sound of the van doors opening. It sounded like more than two people were in the van, but one's mind does play tricks when some of the sense are deprived. Then there was the distinct scent of leather. I knew that Trey wasn't wearing a leather jacket and I don't remember the scent when we entered the van. The engine started, and I worried if they were going to remove the strings on my dick and tits.

I didn't really want to experience the pot holes of the city strung up as I was. But the van was moving and there was no attempt to remove the strings. I was feeling the road surface, man was I feeling it! Then I was shocked out that worry, when what had to be a bag of ice was placed on my naked chest. I jumped and nearly ripped my tits and dick from my body. There was laughter and I could tell that someone had joined the party.

"Hey, don't melt the ice, you're fucking too hot," said a strangers voice. They all laughed.

The ice was removed, as a leather gloved hand wiped the dampness from my body.

The hand was soothing. Then I noticed the strings attached to the tits were cut loose, I moaned appreciatively. But my dick remained tied up. Then another gloved hand was on my body, rubbing my denim legs. The pants didn't move much, they were stuck to my skin. Then two more hands joined in. I now confirmed that there was a third party in the van, since it was still moving and someone had to be driving. They enjoyed watching my body react to their touch, sometimes soft, times with a tickle, time with a pinch or slap. The time passed as touching continued. Then one sat on my chest, it was cool, I could tell they were wearing leather pants or chaps. I was dealing with leather now, another dream coming true. The stranger spoke, sternly to me, "We are going to change the blindfold and gag. DO NOT open your eyes, or speak, or you will be dropped off on the curb immediately!" I could tell he was serious, plus I didn't want to end this now. If it ended now I would forever wonder what was ahead!

The blindfold and gag were removed. I could feel the fresh air touching my sweat covered head and face. I did not open my eyes and didn't speak. I did work my mouth a bit and swallowed in some freshness. Then I felt the gloved hands work their way around my face, head and hair. I wanted to see who this person was, but I was unwilling to end things. I was still spread eagle on the van floor, my dick tied to the ceiling, a leather clad man on my chest driving me wild. He stopped feeling my head, and shortly a leather hood was being worked over my head and covering my head. By the darkness I could tell there were no eye holes. It was stiff, smelled great and was tightly laced up. A gag was strapped up, and it filled my mouth. The laced area was zipped down and a collar portion strapped up, then I heard another zipper and the scent of leather was much stronger. My breathing was warm. I could tell it was one of those hoods that also zipped up into a leather bag. Shit, what was going to happen next? As I thought that, the van came to a stop, the engine turned off.

My dick was released, and stuffed back into my pants, zipper ran up. My shirt was buttoned up, my hands released. I was sat up, my hands cuffed behind my back. A leash was attached to my collar, as my feet were released. Ankle cuffs were locked on.
I was dragged from the van, hobbling as I tried to gain my footing but being dragged along. As I finally got my footing, I found I was carefully led down stairs. I must have been brought to the middle of the room. My hands and feet were released, as I was instructed to remove all my clothing. I did so, fairly quickly, peeling the sticky cloth from my skin. The tit clamps were removed. My only bondage left was my head. I was totally naked and free. I was led a short distance and told that if I needed to piss or shit to do it now. I felt around for a toilet, I was slapped and instructed to do it just standing up. I was also instructed to look straight ahead. It took a bit, but I let go a stream of piss directly in front of me. I could hear it striking the cement and felt it running to my bare feet.

As I finished pissing, I was turned around moving my head

straight but not opening my eyes. The collar, hood and gag were removed. I kept my eyes closed. I was told good boy by Trey. I was now totally free. But that didn't last long. A rubber blindfold was strapped around my eyes, followed by a rubber dick gag, strapped on my face. My hands were cuffed behind my back. Then the power of the shower struck my skin. The water was cold to begin with, they laughed as I jumped and yipped into my gag. But soon it warmed up and was quite refreshing. Then six hands started to give my body a soapy cleaning. They were taking their time, cleaning the points of my tits, the cracks of my ass, the stiffness of my dick. I was relaxed as much as I had been this entire time. Someone lathered my hair and washed it. Of course there was some pinching and slapping, anything to keep me guessing.

Soon I was pretty much clean and rinsed; it felt really nice to get the soda and piss off my skin. Then I felt something making its way up my asshole. It went in a bit then my ass and bowels were filling with a warm liquid.

"We want our birthday boy nice a clean!" chuckled someone.

I was filling up, and it was getting a bit uncomfortable. Then it was pulled out and I was allowed to release. They decided that I wasn't clean enough, and inserted it again filled up, but a bit slower this time. As I was being filled, I could feel someone doing something with my crotch, and then I heard the buzz of the clippers. The cold steel touching my crotch, and I knew that I was loosing my pubic hair. The second enema was pulled out after the shaving was completed. I released. They felt that I was now clean enough.

The three of them then proceeded to towel dry me, harshly and rubbing me. The towels were cheap and stiff. As I was led back to the center of the room, dried, I realized that I had indeed pissed again as this was all going on. But more over I wanted to shoot my load something awful. It had been hours since we started and well, I have been pretty much hard the entire time. My hands were released. I was handed a pair of pants. They were leather and they felt a bit heavy. I slid them on, but was told not to button them yet. I was then slid into a leather shirt, it fit snugly. Then I put on a pair of what must have been tall biker boots. I tucked the shirt into the pants and buttoned and belted the pants. Next I was handed a pair of gloves, that attached to the sleeves of the shirt. The shirt was tightened by laces in the side. I was then put into a heavier leather jacket that was partially zipped up and belted. My hands were cuffed in front of me and raised and chained to the ceiling. There were straps on my legs that seemed attached to the pants that were tightened a bit and I heard the sound of locks being closed. Someone else started to remove the rubber gag and blindfold, I kept my eyes and mouth closed and silenced. The leather bag hood that I had had on before was returned, the gag also. It was tighter this time, with the zipper front being zipped up and locked. My legs then were bound by straps together at the ankle, thigh, and below and above the knees. My hands were stretched a bit, just enough to get my feet slightly off the floor. My crotch was played with, a panel dropped and my dick sprung out. The rawhide was removed from my cock and balls. My balls were put into a weighted leather ball bag and my cock in a leather sheath, then closed and locked into the pants. Finally, I felt a zipper open on my ass, a finger probed my asshole with some lube, then a butt plug was inserted. I moved to my tip toes as they pushed the plug past my tight hole. It was larger than anything I was use too, but there was no stopping them. My ass was then zipped and locked closed. I heard two of the guys leave, someone was standing before me. When he spoke, I knew it was Trey....

"We wanted you to have a bit of time for yourself. Of course this is all for you. We have a while before the party begins. I'll see you later. But of course, you have no idea when you'll see me," with that, he gave me a slight push and I danced a bit like a puppet. He started up that stairs. I could faintly hear a door shut and lock

I was alone, the smell of leather filling my brain. I could feel the leather against every section of my body. Fuck, this is a birthday alright, I am being reborn! I was really enjoying this birthday, more than I had since I got to go to Farrell's when I was a kid!! But this was much more of an experience! Cause I had been dreaming of this for years! And I was no longer a kid. My arms were starting to get tired being in this position, and I'd have to be careful, cause if I shifted my weight down from being on my tip toes, well, they'd hurt more. They must have turned on the heat in this room, because I was starting to sweat like crazy and well I couldn't move much. I was beginning to feel that plug up my ass. It felt really good, and well my dick would sure love some action. But it was really difficult being encased in the leather sheath. But I would find myself trying to fuck that plug in my ass. I was humping myself; it was hard, having very little support on my feet. I was moaning into the gag, fuck I wanted to explode. I could feel my legs straining to pull apart, my hands tried to break free and reach my dick. But it was no use. The more I would try, the worse it got. I just was not going to be letting loose any time soon. I had no idea how long I was going to wait for the party to begin.

Occasionally I could hear them walking on the floor above, maybe some laughing. But it always sounded like the three of them. Suddenly, my ears were filled with the sounds of heavy metal music by Judas Priest rocking away. It was loud and I couldn't hear anything but the music. There must have been headphones in the hood. I could no long hear the outside world, nor could I see it, speak to it or touch it. Even my smell was gone, since I was in this leather bag of a hood. The music passed on. Song after song, at times I tried to fuck my ass with the beat. I was getting tired, stiff and sweaty. And I loved the feel of the tightness of my leather bound body. I was not in control of nothing.

I spent nearly two hours strung up in the leather, when my hands were finally released from above my head. The music did not stop and nothing else was released. The three of them lifted me up and carried me to a table. It was a very strange sensation. I could hear nothing but the music, knew nothing in advance and couldn't move. I was helpless, and man, I bet they loved that about me! I was laid stomach down on what seemed to be a hard table. They uncuffed my hands and preceded to chain them out from my body and must have been chained to the ceiling. My legs were released from the straps and pulled apart.

At this point I started to have an idea where this was headed. My legs were chained wide open, again to the ceiling. The table was then declined a bit, my head being higher than my legs, but only slightly. I could feel straps being put around my torso. I was being securely fastened to this very small table. My crotch area was unlocked and opened. My dick was fished out, as were my balls. A weight was added to the end of the dick sheath pulling my dick. The weighted bag was removed and a parachute was added with some weights attached. Someone started them swinging. Someone ground their hands into the position of my tits. At least with the jacket on, there was no access to them. The music still pounded my brain. The hood was zipped open and the gag removed. Before I could speak, a squirt bottle was put in my mouth and I was instructed to drink down. I did, the water tasted great! Then it was pulled out and a new gag was installed. It had two rings, one that went in front of my lips and teeth, the other behind it. It was frustrating, since I was unable to close my mouth. I could speak, breath, but just not close my mouth. I started to dribble a bit of drool. The blindfold was left in place. Someone tested the new gag, inserting a gloved finger into my mouth. My hooded head was then, somehow at the top, attached to something that held my head up, I could not put it down. Then my pants at my ass were unlocked and unzipped. They pulled out the butt plug and quickly inserted a dildo that was a bit larger, and it was vibrating. There was no where for me to go, I had to deal with the new sensations, I was being fucked by a motor, I started humping the table, my balls and dick swinging below me. The music stopped. Then I heard the voice of Trey.

"Happy birthday! We are here to celebrate and have a great time! I've been planning this for a long time, you have been a great friend and you deserve this so much. I give you this with love."

Then it was silent. Then I heard it. My heart started pounding, I was going where I had never imagined I could. I heard them coming down the stairs, the sound of boots, hitting the wooden steps. I couldn't tell how many there were, but there was more than the three I knew about. When they saw me, there were cattle calls, slang and slurs thrown about like candy. Then I felt their hands touching me. I couldn't count them all, some wore gloves. I could smell the sent of leather, beer, and the distinct odor of man. They were horny men and I was about to be enjoyed by them all!

The dildo was turned off and removed. The hand assault stopped. I could sense someone positioning themselves in front of my face. I knew that I was about to be fucked at both ends, not once, not twice, but a good many times. The time passed by slowly, anticipation. My hands were suspended from me, I couldn't reach anyone. My legs were also useless, my tits were smashed with the clamps against the table, my balls and dick aching as they were be pulled towards the floor and my mouth and ass begging for it all to begin. The headphones crashed the music into the brain, as my mouth and ass were entered at that same time. It wasn't anything slow either; it was quick, violent and hard. I had to work my tongue, keep my body in rhythm as both ends were fucked. Hands were playing with my dick, balls, fingers feeling every inch of my body. I couldn't hear the guys as they were enjoying my holes, but I am sure they were voicing their pleasure.

As one was finished, the other would fill my hole, I was never empty. They never came in me, always pulling out just in advance. The music helped me to keep tempo. My crotch was swaying with the beat, as it pulled on my balls. I wanted to release but the pressure was so strong in the weights, there was no way it was going to happen. My tits felt as if they were going to be ripped right off, as they were ground into table with my moving body. Hands were slapping me, pinching, stroking. Another set of guys would fuck me, then other. After a while I couldn't tell if there were just different guys, or that they were doing me over and over. I was hot, literally and figuratively. I was sweating like a pig, the strong odor of sweat, cum, and beer were filling the room and my nose. The music played on and on....

I swear that at least twenty songs passed by. Then my ass was filled with a butt plug, it just slid right in. The harsh gag was removed and a dick gag inserted. The hood was zipped up again. My pants were sealed again. The weights removed from my dick and balls then they were enclosed into my pants. My feet and arms were released, I just lay upon the table, not moving. The music stopped. I heard the men singing happy birthday to me. Then each one stepped by me, swatting my plugged ass, then headed up that stairs. At last I could count, I was swatted 13 times. I was gang fucked by 13 guys and one of them was my friend Trey. What a friend.

As the last guy left, someone helped me to stand. I was stiff and sore, but I wouldn't mind reliving the night over again. I was lead to a soft bed and laid down on my back. I heard Trey's voice, tell me to lay there and rest. He went up the stairs. I was not restrained, but as I tried, I couldn't get to my dick. My crotch was locked, and I now found out why my legs had straps, there was no way to get these damn pants off. I was truly locked up in leather. I tried to take the hood off, to find it was also locked. I tried again with the butt plug to fuck myself to orgasm. But it was not to be. I was exhausted, so I just settle down, with a raging hard on and remembered the times I had just experienced.

I must have dozed off, because when I awoke, I was disoriented from the hood. My hard on was still with me. Someone was helping me sit up. I was taken from the bed. The leathers were unlocked and removed from my body. I could feel the cool air strike my sweat covered body as each piece was removed. To the end, the last piece to be removed was the hood, gag, and blindfold. Before me was Trey, smiling. My butt was still plugged, tits still in clamps, and my dick and balls still confined, but I was totally naked before him.

"How are you?"

I reached over and gave him a hug so tight and strong. I could never repay him for what he had given me. We pulled apart.

"You better get dressed, so we can get you home." he pointed to my clothes on the floor, still soiled with piss and soda, but with a new element. For I now learned where those guys finally came. My clothing had been laid out on the floor, inside out and that is where they all came. I looked at Trey, he grinned an evil grin. He shoved me over the to clothing and I began to put it on. I could feel the cold, drying cum come between me and my jeans, my shirt, and even in my boots. I packed my bound cock and balls into my jeans, tightened up the belt and told Trey I was ready. He came to me, handed me the leather jacket. I put it on, zipping it up, followed gloves. He cuffed my hands behind my back. Put a leather blindfold and gag on me, then I was strapped into a full face motorcycle helmet. I couldn't see. I was led up the stairs and out into the garage.

Someone else took a hold of my arms and led me to a motorcycle. I could feel the bike seat press against my bound crotch. Someone sat before me; my hands were uncuffed then cuffed around the waist of the rider. I heard the engine start and we raced out of the garage. I couldn't sense where we were going. It was the strangest sensation yet. We rode for what seemed to be an hour or more. The butt plug was ground into my ass on every bump. I know he was racing at high speeds, I felt totally helpless! Then we stopped. My cuffs were undone, my hands cuffed behind my back. I was led up some stairs and to an elevator. I could tell we were returning to Trey's. But Trey didn't know how to ride a cycle. Someone else was bringing me home. We walked out of the elevator, and down the hall and into Trey's apartment.

My hands were uncuffed, and I was instructed to remove my clothing. It was truly sticky now. And my clothing was stiff, since the cum had dried. I was naked and laid on the bed. I was tied down spread eagle once again with the helmet still on my head. Then I heard the door shut and I knew the stranger had left. Trey came to me, "I'm going downstairs to wash and dry your clothing. It will take me a while. You have a project to complete. While I am gone, you are to free yourself and make yourself cum. I don't care how you do it or how long it takes. Just do it. And so you know. That if I return after cleaning your clothes and you haven't cum. Well, I will dress you and send you on your way." with that, I heard the door shut.

I struggled, damn, they had tied me good. This was going to take a while. My cock pointing straight in the air waving around. After a good twenty minutes, I finally got one hand free, and then worked the other. I worked the helmet off, followed by the gag and blindfold. I laid back and reached for my dick. I removed the sheath and ball bag. I left my ankles tied and the plug up my ass. I worked my self, I tried to hold it off, but it came with an explosions and a feeling I've never had. I gushed all over myself, it felt great, I kept working and I'd be damned if I didn't continue to cum. I had never shot so much in my life. It was great, what a great evening. I rested on the bed. Looking for a clock, I was amazed at the time. It was 3am. I had arrived at Trey's at 4pm.

I had been in bondage and someone's mercy for 11 hours. Then I saw it, a video camera was set up, taping me. I couldn't believe it. There was a video record of my birthday.

Trey returned shortly after I undid my remaining restraints. I pulled out the plug and got dressed. He presented me with a tape. The entire night's activities had been taped, for me to relive. I couldn't thank him enough. We hugged for several minutes. I had to be at work in the morning, and really hated to go. But we were both exhausted, and needed to rest. I hugged him again, and headed out the door. When I got home that night, I fell asleep watching that tape. Of course it was on my second time watching it. And I did manage to cum a few times during it. What a birthday that would be, for this is all a fantasy....

Under the Tree

The typical London winter gray has given way to a bright crisp Christmas Eve day. Rolling over in my bed, my morning hard on is trapped in the yellowed jock that Master has me wear. Reaching down, I stroke it a little thinking of spending my first Christmas being collared by the hot Skinhead that picked me up in the Hoist last spring. He has changed my life and is expecting me to move in with him in the coming months.

Stroking, I think about how he had me take a motorcycle training class as he wanted me to start riding a cycle. Over the months he has taken more control and that was just one step. He loves riding and has taken me as pillion several times, him in his full leathers and boots. I hold on to him as we ride and reach around play with his pierced dick through the thick leather. When I do, he speeds up on the M1 and I feel the wind passing my helmet. He has never allowed me to have full leathers; I only get to wear my 14 hole ox blood boots and jeans, along with my bomber and a full black helmet with tinted shield. He did have my helmet marked with the words slave on it and he pisses in it often so that it smells as I wear it. At times it soaks my shaved head, reminding me of the pig I am.

Rolling on my back, I grab one of my boots from the floor and take in the interior boots smell of sweat and leather. After riding, he has me clean his boots and leathers with my tongue as he wears them. He won't allow himself out of them until I am done. By then he is so fucking horny, that he tosses me on the bed and fucks me like the muscled Skinhead he is.

Before I go over the edge and fill the cum crusted yellow jock with more of my sperm, I toss the boot and jump out of bed. Master would be pissed if I shot my load on my own. It is just another thing he wanted to control. Plus I have two hours to get ready and be at his place for Christmas Eve.

After showering, I slide on my rubber shirt and shorts that Master likes me to wear under my skin head gear. Following that with a cock bag in rubber that is locked on, then my red camos, ox blood boots, red FP shirt and maroon bomber, I am ready to head out.

When I arrive, I let myself in. By the door is my rubber hood that I put on immediately. Upon seeing him on the sofa, I go to him, kneeling, putting my hands behind his back; I begin licking the motocross boots that he is wearing. He caresses my head and welcomes me and wishes me a Happy Christmas. I thank him between licks. As I make my way up his boots, he fishes out his cock and balls and presents them before me. As I begin to take them in, he reaches and cuffs my hands behind my back. I then serve him as I am supposed to and want to, with my best. Soon, he is ready to cum. I pull back and he shoots on the crotch of my camos. That means I will have to take them off, but I am not allowed to wash them until I get to my place.

He has me stand, "boy, I want you to go to the bathroom. Take care of all you need to, and then put on what is in the bathtub waiting for you. The key to the cuffs and chastity is there also."

I follow his commands and head to the bathroom. I find the key and struggle for a few moments to unlock the cuffs. But I do get them unlocked and I begin to remove all my clothing, the chastity, including the rubber, but not the hood. I never remove the hood, unless he does so for me. I pee in the boys piss box and seal it tightly. I look into the tub and find a full red rubber suit. As I lift it, I feel the heavy weight of the rubber; I have never seen one like this on before. I work myself into it and find that it is a snug fit all around. The gloves are molded onto the arms, as are the feet. As I enter the suit, I find that the opening is in the back and the hood is attached to the neck. I pull my head up into the hood and find it has clear plastic for the small eye holes, a gag plops into my mouth, with a hose coming out so I can breath. There is a form fitting nose piece that has two small hoses that fill my nostrils slightly. Master comes into the bathroom and seals the opening by zipping then locking it shut.

Master then works my hard cock into rubber fitting that snuggly encases it. I feel a small tube like thing work its way into my piss hole. Then He goes to my ass and a rubber slot is pushed up into my asshole, with a plug. The slot is lined with rubber from the suit. I am now totally sealed from the outside world. Even my eyes are covered in rubber.

He takes me to the living room and before the Christmas tree. He slides me into a complete rubber sleep sack that closes around my neck. He fishes out my cock and attaches a clear rubber tube to it. The tube goes into the hose of a gas mask that is placed on my head after he attaches the tube to the gag. He then adds straps to the sack to make it even more restrictive. The mask is wrapped in red tape. This tape covers my entire body. Finally, he lays me beneath the Christmas tree, leaving me with my sight, but that is really my only sense. Still in his waders, he sits on my chests and I see his smiling face through the two layers of plastic.

"Boy, I told you not to get me a material item for Christmas, didn't I? That is because you are my present...you are all I could want. And I will show you more joy in the next two days than you could have ever imagined. I know that you will have something for me on Christmas Day. I have learned that about you, boy. That is why you are beneath my tree, you are my present. But that doesn't mean I don't have some gifts for you. I do, and I have to go get them today. I know you enjoy your place under my tree. Enjoy the day boy."

With that Master leaves my sight. With the restrictions upon me, I can't follow where he goes. All I see before me is the lights of the tree, the decorations and the bubbles of the bubble lights. My hearing is very slight, but eventually I hear the door shut and feel that he has left for the day.

He is right in that I have planned on what I was going to give him for the holiday. I have already given him some of me, now it was time to give him more. Was this what he was looking for, the time when I would turn myself over to him completely? Am I ready for this moment? I want to make him happy; I enjoy his company and serving him. We have enjoyed our times together very much. Perhaps this is the best present I can give.

Because I am so relaxed in my bondage, I doze off on occasion. During the time, I notice the lightness of the sunny day begin to fade and night fall. Time passes on and on. Eventually I have to piss and do so, drinking it in. I am feeling the plug in my ass big time as it is stretching my asshole and pressing on my prostate. The bottom of the rubber sleep sack is filling with sweat and it allows me to slide around in it

Sometime later, Master appears over me in his full rubbers. "It is Christmas Eve boy." I see a smile through his hood then feel something against my rubber cock. It is a vibrator.

The movement of the rubber slides on my hardening dick. Moaning through the gag, I lift my waist to create move friction on my dick. His rubber booted foot pushes me hard against the floor and I am left to just be pleasured by the wonderful feeling of the vibrator.

I hear duct tape pulled from the roll and the vibrator is secured to my dick.

As I am pleasured with the smooth vibrations, I look up at the lights on the tree, though the plastic covering my eyes from my hood, through the gas mask I notice that the room has grown dark. Have I been enjoying myself so much that I have lost track of time? The days end quickly in the winter and the cold will be settling in for the evening.

I don't know how long I have been under the Christmas Tree on this Christmas Eve.

All I do know is that I was where I have longed to be for many years. I'm in the service of a great man that cares for me more than anyone I have even met. And the more we learn about each other, the stronger our commitment grows.

Then I feel the vibrator increase in speed against my rubber encased cock and balls...I struggle in my cocoon of rubber and tape. I moan through my gag. Soon the piss begins to flow, for I've needed to piss for so long the vibrator removes any holding back that I've been able to do. My ears are suddenly filled with loud SKA music, then the plug in my ass begins to vibrate and finally Master puts tape over my eyes. Every sensation in my body is active; I am going nuts, for I am totally helpless. I struggle in this new rubber suit, which has been secured with tape. My mouth fills with my own piss, and I breath out the tubes in my nose through the gas mask...I am truly a slave to my Master, he controls every part of me.

I want to shoot my Masters load from my dick so much, but he has set the vibrator in just the right position to just give me enough stimulation to want to do it, but not enough to actually do it. This torment doesn't end, it continues, for minutes, then what seems like hours...I have never been this close to the edge before. It is frustrating, painful and wonderful all at the same time. I sweat like a pig, rolling back and forth on my side trying to find relief from this attack. But it moves with me, the sweat in the sack waving along with me. The rolling shoves the plug in deeper and it makes me harder. Not even noticing it, I am humping my own ass with the plug. Though I can't hear much because of the blaring SKA, I swear it hear the laughter of my Master in the room.

I try to track the time through the length of the songs and CD's but they start to repeat, and I loose count. For all I know, I've been through this ordeal for hours. Finally it all stops, very suddenly. All is quiet. I begin to feel my mouth fill with warm piss, but I am not pissing. Then it dawns on me, it is Master's piss. This is one of my gifts to him; I take another step closer to total submission and take in his piss, totally proud to do so.

The tape is removed from my eye pieces, I see Master above me. "Boy, you have given me a great gift tonight. Sleep tight and image what Master Santa will bring you in the morning." With that, the tree lights are unplugged and the room goes dark. I don't know how late it is, but I know that is must be 10 or 11 or later at night, that means I've been a captive in this rubber and tape for nearly 12 hours now. I panic a little, trying to call Master through the gag. He has never left me bound over night. I want to lay with him in his bed. I struggle in the bondage trying to move towards his bedroom. As I try to lift my head, I am stopped by a chain. I realize that the chain is secured to the wall and locked to a ring in the collar around my neck. I trying moving again, but give up so that I do not chock myself to death.

I lay back, looking at the ceiling of the dark room. As my eyes adjust to the darkness, I begin to make out some writing on the ceiling. It is on paper taped to the ceiling. It reads, "U R Fucked. U R Owned. U R slave!"

This only served to make me harder again. Without warning, the headphones came alive with my Master's voice.

"Slave. Get use to the name, for you are now my slave. Before you fall asleep helpless under my tree, I need to share with a phone call. I want you to hear it for you will sleep with it in your head tonight and know from this moment on, I control all in your life."

There is the sound of some static then the voice of my boss at work.

"Sean, really sorry to hear that you have resigned. You meant a great deal to this company. I hope all goes well in your new endeavor! I forwarded the address you sent for your final pay and you will receive it in a week. Cheers!" The phone line goes dead.

Fuck! I have just heard that I have resigned from my job of 8 years! As I want to scream through my gag, I feel so helpless. I hear my Master's laugh in the headphones then another crackle and another phone call.

"This message is for Sean. We received your paperwork and would like you to start on Monday in the New Year! We've assigned you to the cleaning crew at Upper Thames Street waste transfer station. We'll have your gear ready for you. See you then and Happy Christmas!"

I struggle in my helpless rubber bondage, really sweating now as my life is changing without any control. I hear my Master's voice.

"You are fucked, you are owned, you are my slave!"

I scream in the gag and I receive a heavy electric shock from the anal plug. I struggle and squirm in my rubber cocoon. Helpless, he really is showing me that I am owned by him. I realize my dick is hard as a rock. I want to shoot something bad. The shocking continues and the pain is increasing. I roll on my stomach; press my cock into the floor. I push face into the carpet and stop air coming into the mask. Realizing I am like a helpless worm, I stroke harder and harder before I black out. Holding my breath, I feel one huge shock and it reminds me of whom I serve. I am not suppose to jack off on my own, but I am so close.

But I quickly roll on my back and take in the pain to stop my erection.

I try not to feel my rubber encased body, the sweat that I soak in, tightness of the restrains. I look up at that ceiling again and take in the words, focusing on the final one, slave.

Eventually, I fall asleep.

Sometime in the night I am awakened. My mouth is filling with piss again, but it is not mine. I see a shadow of a bearded man lean over me. He smiles at me, through my grogginess, I take in the piss and as the man steps away, I realize it is Santa? He toys with my tits and rubber covered dick for a while. I hear a deep chuckle as I struggle in my rubber and tape. Then he stops tormenting me and I listen very quietly. I never hear a door or any sound. I continue to listen for the longest of time, and never hear a thing. Eventually I fall asleep.

The next time I am a wake, the tree is lit and the sun if filling the room. Master is over me in his skinhead kit, smiling at me.

"Happy Christmas slave".

I try to respond back, but the gag in my mouth makes for a mumbled response. He shows me some scissors and begins to cut the tape from my body. Soon I am loose and he removes me from the rubber sack. I stretch as much as I can. I then kneel before him, facing his crotch. I want to give him a great present; I want to take him in my mouth. But he does not remove the hood yet.

"Slave, I am going to remove the hood in a moment, then I want you to drink the water and juice I have for you. Then I will put your other hood on you and I will let you give me my present." He follows what he said he would do. I enjoy the refreshing taste of the apple juice and the coolness of the water. He then puts on me a full leather hood that has eye, nose and mouth holes. He sits on the sofa and I go to him and take Master's cock into my mouth. I love the smell of his unwashed body and want to eventually lick the great 20 hole boots he has on. His hands rub my leather covered head and rubbery body as I serve my Master.

After a good hour, he comes to his climax and he shoots for the first time in my mouth. We have been together for a great deal of time and we are both safe, this I show him that I am further His boy and put all my trust in Him. I swallow his cum. He takes me to him and hugs me deeply, I nearly cry.

"Slave, you give the greatest gift a Master can receive. I have some special things for you also." He directs me to several boxes under the tree. These were not there before I was secured for the night. Master instructs me which one to open first, when opened I find a full set of race motorcycle leathers. It is a one piece suit, in black and red, with full armor. He has me remove my sweaty rubber and put on the leathers. They feel so heavy and wonderful against my skin. The next box has a pair of black motocross boots. As I am instructed to put them on, I enjoy the feel of the leather and plastic. The next box is a full face helmet, red and black that matches the leathers. I put it on; the shield is mirrored, creating a mysterious look. The final box has a pair of black race gloves that Velcro tight on the wrists. I am now looking like a cycle guy, a dream come true. Master then leaves for a moment and comes back dressed in his black leather jacket, jeans, chaps, boots and carries a helmet also. He leads me to the garage and in the garage is a brand new Suzuki sport bike, in the same red and black of my leathers. Master turns me around to face him.

"Slave, today I give you a gift, and take control of your life. Beginning today you will only ride that bike to your new job. No matter the weather, you will ride a cycle. We will be putting together gear for you to ride, including rain gear. Of course if it snows, you won't be riding, but you don't go to work in the snow anyway."

"I'm having you do this, because a car is too good for a slave. It is comfortable. On a motorcycle, you will always feel the power of your Master between your legs. Since you always wear chastity or cock devises, you are going to feel them. Plus you will always be in leather, and I guarantee you will have rubber on under your leathers. As you do now.

You will also wear rubber to work. You have been assigned to the crew that cleans the rubbish trucks. You will be wearing a full rubber suit over your work gear, which will be over your body rubber and chastity. Your boss is a mate of mine and he understand you're a bit queer. Most cause you'll be wearing you full leathers while working. And that helmet will always be worn with a hood, including at work. So guess you'll be locked in that hood many, many hours a day. The others at work might think you're a bit of freak, but I don't fucking care. They shouldn't talk to you anyway. You're job is to clean those trucks and get you ass back home. On your knees, slave."

I lower to my knees, feeling the pucks from the leather suit. Putting my gloved hands behind my back, I look up at my Master through the shield of my helmet.

"I own you because I love you. You serve and worship me because you love me. You will do anything I command, no question. You are fucked, you are owned, you are my slave!"

He brings my helmeted head to his crotch and rubs it against his bulging cock.

"Get on your bike. Remember when we both go riding, you will always ride behind me, because that is where my slave belongs."

As I climb on my crotch rocket, he climbs on his bike, putting on his helmet. The garage door opens and we race down the driveway and into the street. This Christmas Day is going to be in my mind forever, for we each received gifts that the other really wanted the other to have.

Inescapable

It was an awesome day out. The sun was shining and the temp was nearing 80. I could no longer sit in front of the computer and work on the web site. So I put on my biking gear, loaded the bike into the car and headed down the highway. I ended up on the Cedar River where they have converted the train tracks to a bike trail.

I put on my helmet and gloves and started my ride. Eventually, after several hours, the blacktop trail turned to gravel. I was feeling very ambition today, so I continued down the trail. I had to be about ten miles from my car now, and even further from the city. This was the country alright. There was hardly a sound, except for birds and the river.

The smell of the spring flowers was strong and the light green of everything was refreshing. I hadn't passed anyone on the trail since it turned to gravel. I guess not many actually take the trail this far up.

The sound of nature was broken by the distant noise of motocross or dirt bikes. I guess they could use the trail too, since I never saw any signs restricting them. I continued on. Soon, I could tell the bikes were heading up behind me. I slowed down and let them pass. They were in full MX gear and it looked great! I love the boots, helmet, gloves, pants, and plastic that MX riders wear. There was some movement in my crotch was they headed up the trail. But being in my spandex bike shorts, there wasn't much room for a hardening dick.

I waited for the dust to clear and then continued up the trail. The trail had long ago left the main street that paralleled it. It was great to be alone out in the woods. It was a week day, and I began to think of how my Master would have loved this bike ride also. And well, the advantages of being self employed allowed me to get out and enjoy the great day. My thoughts turned to Master again. He is a really great man, and I have been in his service for a while now. A bike ride like this wouldn't have been possible without his guidance of getting me into better shape. I'm down in weight and well, I can wear a 34 pant, and I look good without my shirt, which is something I would have never done in the past. Sir has taken me to the bars a few times, in just my leather pants and boots, no shirt and of course, wearing my collar.

I enjoy it when the other Masters just look at us. I know I make Sir proud to show me off. At the bar, we are always together. He isn't afraid to hold me, I love to feel his gloved hand on my shaved head. Sometimes he gets a little rough with me and toys with my tits, or I will kneel before him and clean his boots. I enjoy it all, I like making the other boys jealous that they aren't serving a great Master like I am. And I like making the other Master's jealous, for they could've had me but weren't patient enough to work with me and find the true boy inside.

As the trail progresses, there is an old train bridge ahead. It is pretty high over the river. As I start to cross it, I hear the sound of one of the dirt bikes and ahead of me, the guy on the bike comes up on the trail and blocks the path. I continue to pedal but slow down. He waves for me to come forward. I am getting a bit nervous. What the hell is going on? I stop in the middle of the bridge. I don't want to show them that I am afraid of them. But I don't want to get into any trouble either. Just then the other biker appears on the opposite end of the bridge. This is not what I had planned for the day. I was a bit apprehensive but also, I am getting excited. These guys have the gear and they are hot looking. With the full face helmets and mirrored goggles I can't see their faces. The one before me yells to me to come to him. I decide that short of jumping off the bridge there isn't much I can do. I ride up to him and stop. He turns off his bike, as the other rider rides his towards me. Looking at them both, I am thankful for the padded bike shorts, they won't be noticing my hard on that is growing.

"What are you doing?" the Rider before asks. I tell him that I'm just riding this trail. "Well, there is a fee for this trail, did you pay it?" he asks. I had never heard of a fee and didn't see where to pay it.

"The fee is that you are gonna suck us off, both of us." his comment surprises me. "You're a faggot boy if I ever saw one. So you won't mind doing this!"

"I can't do that for you…I will pay your fee some other way, but I can't have sex with you", I respond. He asks why and I tell him that I am only allowed to serve one man and I am committed to him. They start laughing, and then one notices the chain and lock around my neck. He reaches for it with his gloved hand.

"You're a slave boy aren't you?" I nod yes. "Damn, this is our lucky day!" he pulls the chain around my neck closer, my face nearly pressed against his helmet. "Listen boy, we're all going down this bank and you're gonna suck us off and since we know you're a slave boy, we might even fuck your ass and play with you all afternoon. And what are you going to do about it?" I stare into his goggles, wondering what this asshole thinks of me and why he thinks he can get away with this. His partner slaps my head with his gloved hand.

"What do you say boy?" I can't believe the words come out of my mouth but they do. "Nothing Sir, I am yours Sir"

I am pulled off my bike and set on the back of the Honda. They both ride down the embankment and under the bridge. There is a dirt road and two pick ups parked next to the river. One is a nice new Dodge Ram with a canopy, the other is an older Ford, and I suspect that is how they haul the bikes. They get off their bikes and order me to stand against the support of the bridge. I am scared, and well, I am also excited. These guys have the gear that I would love to be wearing. But I am scared, because they don't respect my dedication to Master. I know if he was here, he would be protecting me against these jerks. One grabs some rope from the back of the Dodge, I think of him as Red, because that is the color of his helmet. The other is wearing a Blue helmet. Red comes to me, tells me to face the support and before I know it, my hands are tightly tied behind my back. He turns me around and orders me to kiss his MX boots. I look down to see them standing in the wet dirty, almost muddy ground. I hesitate, but he slaps my face with his gloved hand. "Do it!"

I have no choice, I must obey, if fall to my knees in the mud and kiss his boots. He laughs just a little.

He then orders me to clean them. They are very dirty and a bit muddy. Plus my mouth was a bit dry from the bike ride. It is very difficult to get into the buckles and other areas of the boots. While I clean his boots I'm not sure what Blue is doing. Then I see my bike fly off the bridge and land in the water. As I finish the boots, Red lifts one and pushes me against the support and wipes the mud on the bottom of the boot on my T-shirt and then my face. He orders me to stand and then takes my bike shorts off, followed by my underwear. I can no longer hide my excitement of this moment. Red looks down at my hard dick, pointing straight at him. "Fuck, he loves what I'm doing to him!!"

Blue, coming down the bank, turns to see my hard dick and starts laughing. "Boy what you enjoying about this?"

"Sir, when you guys passed me in your MX gear that is when I got hard. I am scared, for you do not respect my Master. But I have to admit that I love your gear!"

"You do huh?" I nod my head in agreement.

Red goes to Blue, leaving me standing. They laugh a bit, returning they both take off their helmets. They smile at me. Red speaks, "Boy, I have decided to suspend your fee for the path. But in doing so, I have also decided that you are going to take a new path." Red comes to me and takes the bandanna from around his neck and ties it around my eyes. It is sweaty. A glove is placed in my mouth and another bandanna, most likely from Blue, is tied to hold it in. I am lead to the truck and I sit on the tailgate. My shoes and socks are removed. Here I am now, naked from the waist down, gagged, blindfolded and my hands behind my back secured.

Just then I feel them dressing me in some pants, then some sweaty socks and boots. It comes to me they are dressing me in the MX gear. They take some laces from my shoes and tie off my cock and balls. My T-shirt is cut off me and my hands are freed. They slide the jersey and chest protector on me, then tuck it into my pants and zip them up.

They laugh as they toy with my now captive cock and balls. I feel the helmet and goggles placed and secured on my head. They push me into the back of the truck. My hands and feet are tied together, and I am in a sort of hog tie. It is very warm in the back of the truck with the canopy, the sun beating down on it. It isn't long before I am sweating in all this gear. I hear the tail gate slam. Some muffled noises work their way to me though the helmet. I figure they are loading the bikes. Shortly, the truck is running and I am getting bounced around in the back. I have no idea where I am going. No one knew I was out on this bike ride. And Sir was supposed to call me this evening. But I am helpless. I hope these guys take me home and then let me go. If I have to have sex with them, I am sure Sir will understand the situation. I hope that I do not ruin his trust and respect for me, for that is the last thing I want to do. When I do get loose and free, I will find these guys and let them face the wrath of my Master. They won't know what hit them!

My head slams into the metal bed of the truck as we came to a quick stop. Thank gawd I am wearing this motocross helmet. But it is still hotter than hell in it. Being blindfolded and gagged makes it worse.

I struggle with the ropes that bind my hands behind me, my legs together in a hog tie. But those dirt bikers did an excellent job at securing me. As we travel to who knows where, I am tossed about in the back of the truck like a rubber ball. Thankfully the gear they put me in has padding, but at times my gloved hands are still crushed by my weight as I roll upon myself. In the bed of this truck, on this summer day, it is like an oven. I feel the weight of the heavy leather boots on my feet, the nylon pants tucked into them, my tied balls inside straining, the long sleeve jersey tucked into the leather gloves, and of course this chunk of plastic holding my head hostage.

I'm not sure these guys know how powerful my Master is, how he will crush them when he finds out about them. Believe me, he will know. This action that they take can not be left unpunished. They knew what my collar meant, yet they still used my submissive state to their advantage. They disrespect my ownership and devotion to my Master, how dare they make me suck them off, their dirty biker dicks. If they wanted my services, then they should have contacted Master and he would've either let me or not. But I am not theirs to use as they please.

But still I can't deny that I am aroused by their power over me. Of course, bondage always makes me very excited. I can't imagine what they might have in store for me, hopefully it will be short and it will all end.

It seems they purposely go around corners, stop and go more quickly so that I am thrown around more. It is a total helpless feeling to be back here, sweating, unable to yell for help, unknown to where they might be taking me. At least I know there is only one, since the other had to drive the truck with the bikes in it. When we stop and he gives me a change by letting mc loose, I will take my advantage!

As my thoughts of escape continue, the truck comes to a halt. But this is longer than normal; I sense the engine is off. But it is difficult to tell with the helmet on. But I do hear the tailgate open. Several items are tossed in, one or two striking me. I moan and jump in my bondage.

"How you doing slave boi?" one asks, pushing his fist into my crotch, smashing my balls. I moan loudly into the gag. With that the tailgate is closed.

"boi, there is to be no sound out of you. I'm back here to toy with our new captive while Trev drives us to our destination. What ever happens, you are not to make a sound. Nothing, fuck head! You got it?!" With that, he slams his boot into my side. I moan, only because it is natural to do so.

"boi, you fucking don't understand," again the boots strikes me! I learn and stay quiet, as the pain shoots through my body.

"Good boi." he pats my cock and balls. "Now let's check out that slave dick of yours." he states as he un-does the Velcro at my crotch and pulls out my bound dick and balls. He twists them in his hands, but I stay quiet. I will not fall to his domination over me. I will remain strong. He starts patting them, almost stinging, then stinging for sure! I struggle in my bondage, but don't moan or scream.

"That's right boi, struggle all you want. Feel how helpless you are, but don't make a noise." he continues this conquest of my balls. He takes the pain a notch higher, I want out of this bondage now. But as I struggle, my dick gets harder, as he notices and reminds me. As I struggle, my feet pull on my arms, and I can't get release. I sweat even more, feeling it run down my face and into the cloth of the gag.

He then ties my dick and balls off to some point in the truck, pulling on them. I am on my side and don't have much balance. As the truck turns, I either roll over on my balls, or pull away the other side stretching. He yells at the driver to swerve some. And it is intense as I wobble back and forth, straining and crushing my own crotch. He laughs, sometimes kicking me as he enjoys seeing me struggle. Once or twice I start to yell, as the pain hits hard, but I hold it in.

Now the pattern of movement seems more up and down. By the noise that I can hear, I can tell we are on a concrete freeway. Damn, where are we going! I feel him reach for the strap on my helmet, working it. The helmet and goggles come off and I feel the warm but fresh air strike my wet head. I feel something shoved into my face and the gag removed.

"You know what to do boi." I smell leather and then realize, his boots are before me. Oh, how can I lick them? I don't respect him and he doesn't deserve that kind of attention. Just then, he strikes my dick hard with something. I jump in pain, almost yelling, as it seems to almost cut my skin. My tongue comes out quickly and I start to lick. He brings his gloved hand down to my neck, pushing my face deep into the leather. As I cover it more and more with spit, my nose and cheeks are covered as they slide around his boot. He turns his boot, since I an unable to reach some parts. I feel it is the sole and taste the dirt and mud. I stop, he strikes my dick again. "Taste it boi, eat it! You slave shit!"

I dig my tongue deep into his soles, tasting the rubber mixed with mud. The constant motion of the truck keeps me bobbing from side to side, but not as much as when we were turning. When I am done with one boot, he shoves his other one in. As I start licking, he starts stroking my dick. I stop with the feeling of possible release. I am kicked in the face, "Fuck no, don't stop boi!" he hells at me.

I start right away. The sensations are building in me. I am tied totally helpless in motocross gear; he has secured my cock and balls, stretching them, as I lick his dirty leather boots. He works my dick over and over, I get near. He can tell by my breathing.

"boi, if you shoot your load in this truck, you're dead meat." I am struggling to hold it in. I am so close. He whips me with the things across the dick, the pain bringing me back to reality. Over, over and over he whips, I feel my dick must be getting cut. It takes me out of my pleasure trance and brings me back to pain and submission. He notices it and laughs.

He pulls his boots out of my face, gagging me and putting the helmet back on me. I hear the sound of duct tape and he tapes my goggles securely. Then his boots slam my head down. "boi, we own you. You are ours to do as we fuckin' please." He slams me down again with his boot.

He begins to release my boots and hands from their bondage. It feels wonderful to feel the freedom and stretch my legs. He leaves my hands tied behind my back. Taking my feet, he secures them to the top of the camper shell. Lying heavily on my back, crushing my hands, I feel him tape them together. He tapes my ankles, then knees. I feel the nylon and leather together against my skin, the sweat running down to my open crotch. Then a wider surface is binding me. After a bit, I can tell it is plastic wrap. Fuck! He is going to mummify me, I just know it. He begins wrapping, layer after layer, as it gets tighter and tighter. I struggle a bit, he knows that I am scared, but knows there ain't anything I can do about it. Then the sound of the tape again as he covers ever inch of my feet and legs. He goes right up to my crotch and stops. He lowers my legs with a thud to the bed of the metal truck.

Then taking some rope, he wraps it around my neck, sitting me up and securing it to the ceiling of the shell. If I move too much I choke. He releases my hands, and before I can do much, he has taped them to my sides. I don't dare moan at this point, for I don't know what his plans are and I need to be on his good side. The plastic wrap begins at my waist, tight and many layers build up my body, around my neck and over the helmet. Soon, my breathing becomes difficult because he has me totally covered in plastic. I feel it move in and out with each breath. I hope that he will open an air hole soon, and he does. I breathe easier. Then he starts with the tape, around, making each inch tighter and me more helpless.

He covers my neck and up to my head. I must look like a silver mummy by now. Through it all he leaves my dick and balls exposed. They have gone limp for I am now scared more than horny. He releases the rope and I fall hard to the floor. Once again, I am thankful for that helmet.

In all his work, I feel that the truck has come to a stop. I hear the tailgate open and them both talking. They start moving me around, pushing me towards the tailgate. I feel that I am at the edge. "boi, this is where you get off!" I am shoved from the gate and land hard in the dirt. I can tell because it is softer than pavement.

"We're in the middle of nowhere boi, no one knows where you're at, and we don't really care." I am kicked in the stomach. "We're out of here! Good luck slave boi, hope your Master finds you before the bears!" I struggle, starting to yell into the gag. There are no repercussions for doing so. I hear the truck start, fuck they are leaving me here! The engine noise fades away. I lay very still; I hear nothing, not a damn thing. I am totally secured in plastic, tape, gagged, sightless in where I don't know.

I struggle in this cocoon that I'm in. But as I do I sweat even more. The top of this plastic and tape seem warmer, I must be lying in the direct sun. I do manage to get myself to roll on my stomach, but only find that it is more difficult to breathe that way. So, with a great deal of effort, I roll over on my back. I can wiggle my fingers in the gloves, but he taped my wrists so securely there is no way to get them free. I can feel the beads of sweat rolling from my head, into my eyes where they pool. What if they leave me here forever, I will surely die. Of course I can hope that evening will arrive soon and things will cool down.

If only Master knew what they have done to me. Master, He will be arriving home and not finding me there. He will be very upset and I will be punished. How can I explain what these guys did to me? I can only hope Master will not punish me greatly, once he allows me to explain what happens. I know that Master is very considerate of my feelings and He would never punish me for a situation that was out of my control. But at the same time, I knew I wasn't supposed to be out riding my bike without letting Him know my plans for the day. I would think that after three years of serving Him I wouldn't try to hide things from Him. Perhaps I deserve what is happening.

No, I can't think that way. What has happened is totally wrong. They have no right to use me as their sex slave. If they should come back, I will not serve them sexually at all. But, if I don't, will I be disappointing Master? They are dominating me, so Master would want me to submit to the more powerful. He has been proud of me in the past when I have done so. I will do what they want. There is also a survival factor, for if I do as they want, they might let me go. And my goal should be to do what ever it takes to get back to Master as soon as possible.

Time passes, it is getting unbearably uncomfortable in my bondage. The shirt I wear has soaked up sweat until it is wet. The pants are nylon so the sweat just seems to be pooling in them. On occasion I get hard, but most of the time I'm not. This is not enjoyment at this point. I try to rest, for it is the only thing I can do. I don't know what time of day it is.

My slumber is awakened when a sharp pain fills my chest, then another. Shit, someone is punching my chest. There is slam on the helmet making my entire body shake.

"Fuck boi, wake up!" I hear the familiar voice. They have returned. As I wake more, I feel very strange; there is no weight on my body. I'm not lying on my back, or could it be that I am numb? My head is feeling heavy though. Then I feel a hand on my crotch and I feel movement. Finally I wake enough to know that I am hanging upside down. My feet and ankles are tighter. "boi, you're hanging like a side of beef!" Soon the tape is cut away from the goggles and I see before me their boots! I am in the woods, where, I couldn't know. One of the boots comes up and kicks my helmet and I begin to sway uncontrollably.

They walk over to their bikes that I can see in the distance, climbing on. Starting them up, they rev them. Then I see them both pick up a cattle prod. I know what they look like, because Master has used one in the past. I can only hope that the plastic, tape and gear I wear will protect me. One races off behind me. I can't move my head, but soon see the other racing for me. As he gets close, he holds out his arm and Fuck! I feel the shock as he strikes me. I sway on the rope, spinning, soon another, as the other rider strikes me. I watch as the forest spins around me. This is totally helpless, what they do to me. They turn around and come back, again and again! I am shocked over and over, where ever they can as they ride by. Since they aren't wearing helmets, I see the big grins on their faces. I struggle in the bondage, as they race by again, screaming into the gag! One stops his bike, as my face passes within inches of his back tire, he roosters a bunch of dirt and rocks at me. Then he races off.

By the time they tire of this game, I am weak and helpless. I struggle not at all, and their fun is over. I am lowered to my back. Shortly the tape and wrap is removed and I feel the cool of the forest air striking my wet body. They walk me over to a tree and have me kneel against it, with my back to it. My hands are tied behind me around the tree, as are my booted feet. They remove my helmet and gag. Before I can move my mouth much, one of their dicks is in it. He slams my throat, over and over. Yet I don't gag, because I am well trained. He is close to cumming, pulling out and shoots over my head. I feel it dripping down my neck as he must have hit the tree. I lower my head, but it quickly lifted as the other guy slams his dick in my mouth. He is rougher than the first and takes longer to get to the brink. At times he takes his gloved hand holding it over my nose, watching me struggle with my breathing. But soon, even he is removing his dick and shooting on my chest. I collapse the best I can, tied to the tree. They roughly put a leather hood over my head, snap in the gag. I am lifeless, as they walk away laughing.

Eventually I get some strength back and look around. They have set up a tent and chairs, next to the truck. I notice Red coming to me. He releases the bondage and hands me a jug of water. He removes the gag, I take a sip, and then he orders me to drink it all down.

When I am done, he snaps the gag back in, then grabs me by the shirt and drags me to a point in front of the camp they have constructed. I see before me a staked out area with string. He hands me a shovel and tells me to start digging. As I start digging, with what strength I pull from deep inside me. I begin to worry that I might be digging my own grave. I am stopped and Red puts a gas mask over my hooded head, removing the gag. It has a hood that he draws tight. A hose dangles from the front of the mask. He tells me to continue digging.

In the full motocross gear, I am digging a hole. My breathing is heard strongly by me, as I intake and outtake via the hose. The hole gets deeper, and as I look at it, it is about three feet wide by 7 feet long. It is the size of a body, my body. Why would they want to kill me?

I can't believe I continue to dig. I should just stop and let them dig the hole after I am gone. But I guess it is the side of me that believes I'm going to live. I will not let them take me. That is a boi with confidence talking, something Master has instilled in me from day one.

As I dig, they sit on the chair watching, drinking beers. Sometime the verbally humble me, other times just converse as if I wasn't there.

Finally after I have dug to about a foot over the top of the motocross boots I wear, they order me to stop. I am led to a fallen tree and again roped over it. The MX pants are released and pulled down. "Now for you to learn the true power, fuck boi," with that someone puts his dick near my ass. Slowly he works it in, but once in, he slams it in and out. I yell into the gas mask. As I do, the hose is blocked!

"Silence or I will silence you," so with that I take their fucking power in silence. He is strong with me and soon I hear his moan, knowing he is getting close. But he doesn't pull out. "This time you take it boi," I am devastated as he shoots his load in my ass! How can he degrade me so! For I am a slave, but only take my Master's cum in my ass! I struggle to get free; I want to hurt this Man for doing this to me. But as I struggle, he pulls out and is quickly replaced by his partner. The more I struggle, the harder he fucks me. I eventually give up and let him have the control he has over me. This guy takes forever to reach is climax, but he does and eventually pulls outs. He slaps my ass hard, and then slams a butt plug in there. I hear them walk away, as I rest on the fallen tree.

It is getting dark in the forest, as they come to me. They release the ropes; stand me up and pulling the MX pants up. They walk me to the pit that I have dug. Standing me in the middle, they take the duct tape and tightly tape my ankles, then my knees and thighs. They tape my gloved fingers together, then put them in a fist and tape them into a ball. My hands are placed at my sides and tape wrapped around my wrists and body, elbows and body and upper arms. Tape is wrapped around the neck of the gas mask hood. I struggle as they begin to lower me into the pit.

I am laid on my back, straight. Then they both pick up shovels. My heart begins to race as they dig those shovels into the pile of dirt from the pit. As the dirt falls on my body, I scream into the gas mask. I struggle and wiggle about as I have never in my life, as they load pile upon pile of dirt upon me. The weight begins to measure against me; they don't stop, as I can struggle less and less. They are burying me alive!

One stops and looks at the extreme fear in my eyes, and laughs, "Where is your Master now slave? Looks like we own you!" He tosses a load of dirt on my head, it slides off the shield of the gas mask.

Faster than when I dug it, they are filling the hole. I am a good two feet under the dirt, it weights against me. I still try to get loose, but it is no use. The dirt makes its way up my body until I feel it closing in around my head. They both work as the dirt covers the shield, I scream over and over! I fall into darkness and the weight continues to grow, then changes no more. I realize that my only connection to the outside world is the hose on the mask. This is a situation far too intense for me! Master would never do this to me! Never!

Suddenly I smell rubber and dirt, then the air stops. I breathe in and the mask clings to my face. I struggle and yell into the mask. Shortly the air begins. Then the air become labored as I breathe in, then a little drop of moisture, then another and then a rushing of liquid. I discover that if I don't drink it, I will drown. I swallow quickly, the salty, bitter, beer tasting liquid, and then I realize they are pissing in the tube. They have conquered me totally! I get it all down, with the after taste lingering.

I hear a voice, "boi?" Slowly I take it in, as it calls again. "boi, we own you. So you know your Master sold you to us. And now, we are training you! Think of how you will be serving us!"

With that the air is cut off again. I struggle, and then take in the fresh air as it returns. They are lying to me. Master would never sell me! I will survive this! I must survive this!

Moto slave

It was Friday night and things looked great for the weekend. My Master had planned for us to go riding on Saturday, enjoying the great spring weather as a chance to ride the Honda CBR. The weather had been cold and wet lately, so Master hadn't had the time to go out and do the riding he loves. Many times he goes out on his own, because he can rider faster and makes better time without me on the back. But he always says when he gets home that he missed me on back, holding him. I always enjoy seeing him come in the door, in his full black race leathers, pulling his full black helmet off his sweat covered head. After getting water from the refrigerator, he sits in his chair and I immediately take care of his boots. The taste of the leather and some of the road grime fills my tongue and at the moment, I love my position in life, serving my Master, showing him my devotion. Normally, his gloved hand comes down and strokes my shaved head letting me know that I am safe with him for another evening.

My dick has grown, starting to drip as I lower to my knees awaiting Master's arrival home from work. I am in my leather pants and 14 hole boots, shirtless, with the collar locked around my neck. I wait for him to enter the door, as I hear his truck pull in the drive. Putting my hands behind my back, I lower my head as he opens the door.

I smell the fresh air and sweat that covers his Carhartts and work boots, as he enters. Closing the door, I look up at him, he smiles, bending down and kissing me fully on the lips, his tongue making its way down my throat. I can tell this is going to be a good night. His hand reaches my collar and pulls me away from his lips down to his crotch and he holds my head there, tasting the dust on his stiff gold Carhartts. I feel his hard dick inside wanting it so, but knowing we have dinner to eat, then the rest of the night. Keeping my head to his crotch, he walks to his chair and sits. He strokes my shaved head with his bare, but dirty hands, at times driving my head deeper into his crotch.

"Take it out, beautiful boi," is his first words since arriving home. After being together for the past two years, I know what he means. I work the zipper with my tongue and teeth, eventually pulling it down. Easier, is releasing his dick into freedom. He grabs my ears and drives his dick into my mouth, filling it. The warmth I know he feels, for he moans slightly. Then there is a trickle, and then it rushes down my throat. I pull back briefly, but he holds me tight, as he pisses in my mouth. I take it in easily as I have had practice often and know this is his comfort to do so.

He pulls me off quickly and finishes pissing on my chest. This is not normal for him to do so, but I accept it. Then his voice changes as he challenges me, "boi, why did you pull back?"

"Sir, I'm sorry. I was surprised a bit."

He doesn't like the answer, he lectures me how I should know better and have been trained to do better. I am now feeling sorry for not being as good as I know I am. I can tell that Master is disappointed in me.

"Dog, to the bedroom," when he calls me Dog, I know I am in trouble and slide into a new mind set. On all fours I follow him to the bedroom. He grabs the leather hood, roughly putting it on my head, and lacing it very tightly. The gag slips in. He points to the cage that sits in the corner of the room. I walk over to it and crawl in. Master secures my feet together and my hands, and then secures my hands over me to the top of the cage. My hardening dick presses against my leather pants. I know I am in trouble, but it is what happens when I am put into bondage. But I know how he is securing me will soon be no longer pleasurable and begin to ache.

"Think about your error, dog," he begins changing out of his work clothes, throwing his boots on the top of the cage for me to stare at. Knowing I need to clean them for the end of the week for him, but I can't.

When he is done changing, he turns out the light and leaves the room, closing the door. Shortly after, I know I have erred and now wish I was more thoughtful. While being with Master for two years, I seldom face this kind of punishment. But when I do, it bothers me greatly, as it does Master. We like touching each other, holding each other. But he knows that he must deny himself and me this pleasure for me to learn my errors. I know he doesn't like it, for he has told me so many times. But I need to learn and learn I do.

Time passes slowly in the dark. As I knew, my dick is no longer hard. But I think of Master, alone, eating his dinner I prepared, and then cleaning the dishes, knowing I should do that. I hope he returns soon, but he doesn't. I begin to think of how disappointed he is in me and that I hope it doesn't ruin our ride tomorrow. But if he goes riding without me, I will understand.

I hear the door open, but the light doesn't come on. I see the silhouette of Master coming towards me; he lowers his sweat pants and begins pissing on me again. Helpless I take it on me, even on my leather. He is silent, and then leaves the room when finished. The warm piss turns cold and I take in the leather, piss smell. This is not normal, and I know that he is really upset. How I want to be able to touch him and let him know I am sorry. But I will be doing that when he allows me to.

I see those boots and know that I should've had them taken care of by now. On the bed lays his work clothes that I should've put away. I start to get sleepy, and close my eyes.

I'm awakened with the wetness striking my chest again. This time Master is naked as he finishes peeing on me. He climbs into bed and rolls away from me. Now I want to be with him. It is very rare, in fact I can't remember when, I was not allowed to sleep with him. I want to say something to him, and try with the gag in my mouth. Startling me, Master jumps from the bed, unlocking the cage. He is going to release me, he misses me also!

He unties my feet, removing my boots and pulling down my leather pants. I can't move for I'm still secured to the top of the cage with my hands. I hear him going through our drawers, and then returning. He spreads my legs and puts a good sized butt plug up my ass. He pulls the leathers back up, belting them, and then shoves the plug in more. Re securing my feet, he locks the cage again and goes to sleep. The plug is large, and hurts. I struggle in my bondage, now feeling very helpless, smelling the piss that covers me and soaks my leather hood. I decide that I'm going to spend the night this way and take it! I need to redeem myself to Master, and doing well this night will be that way.

I wake to find myself sliding out of the cage. My hands have been released from the cage only recently, for they are still stiff. Master sits me up, removes the gag and I know what to do at that point. I reach up and take his dick in my mouth. Out comes the strong morning piss. I do not hesitate; I do it the right way this time. When complete, I tongue his piss slit. He lets me pull back, "I think slave has learned his lesson."

"Yes handsome Master, I have." with that he lifts me up, with my feet still bound and hugs me. The hug I have been craving since he arrived home. When done, he smiles at me, as I look back in his eyes. We love each other something fierce and this brings us closer together.

"boi, go put on your MX boots, shirt, leather jacket, gloves and grab your helmet," he removes the secures around my feet. As I leave the room to where my gear is stored he reminds me to relieve myself also. But walking I remember the plug still in my ass. I will remind him of it before we head out.

I change quickly after taking care of personal matters, loving the feel of the additional leather. I then think about how I am covered with Masters dry piss, as it gets layered in the leather. The hood is still soaked with piss and reminds me of that on occasion with a whiff of the odor.

Master comes into the room, in his full leathers. I stare, knowing how lucky to have a guy this wonderful looking caring for me. I instinctively fall to my knees and kiss his riding boots. That gloved hand falls and touches my head; I reach around and grab his leather covered legs, hugging them, feeling the security in them, the strength that keeps me so in love with him. His hand moves down my leathered back and around my ass. He pushes the plug in to remind me there it is there. I moan and stir a bit.

"Oh, I remember it is there boi. And it stays there until I want it out." I look at him and he just smiles at me. "But Master--", is all I can say before he reminds me of my night in the cage and if I wanted to spend the day there, instead of on the back of his CBR. I was silent.

He produced the gag that attaches to the hood, secured it, then put on my helmet. It is black and full face with a mirrored shield, so no one can see my hooded head. I stand, putting on my gloves and we make our way to the garage.

Opening the door, he puts on his helmet with mirrored lens. He climbs on board, as I do. I feel the plug against the hard seat. I reach around him, holding him as he loves and we ride off.

The feeling of riding in full leather, both of us, hearing it squeak and move on us as we race on the street. When we are open stretches of road, Master pushes my gloved hands to his crotch to toy with his dick through is leathers. He talks of creating a glove and leather suit that would allow greater contact. The glove would attach to the front of his suit and my bare hand would touch his bare dick. As I worked, he would speed faster and faster down a lonely barren road. As he hit his top speed, he would shoot his load on my hand and feel the power of excitement and living on the edge.

It is a warm day and I sweat heavily in my leather covered head in the black plastic helmet. All day we ride, stopping on occasion to check out a site, I can never remove my helmet. I smell the piss mixing with the sweat. I look at others in cars as we ride by, if they only knew of this slave in his leather, gagged, unable to speak to the world, protected by the man in full race gear that my arms wrap around. How I love feeling him, my leathered chest on his leather back. We are as close to each other as we can, going 70 on the open road, the wind rushing past us, as I continue to toy with his dick. Helpless I am, gagged and feeling every bump with the plug up my ass. It is moments like this that make our relationship so strong.

As we ride, time passes and we never track it. As the sun sets, we head back to the city. He pulls the bike into the garage. The door lowers as I climb off the bike. He remains sitting, grabbing my leather jacket taking me to my knees. He removes my helmet, then gag. He points to his boots and I begin licking the road grim from them. As I do so, he cuffs my hands behind my back. I clean the tall leather boots; he even makes sure I do the soles. I feel the heat from the engine, as his boots sit on the pegs. I crawl around to take care of the other boot. When he is happy with my cleaning, he pats me on my head. I rise and he removes the cuffs. He puts the gag back in and returns the helmet.

He bends me over the CBR and secures me, my arms spread. He then undoes my leather pants and drops them as far as he can, then ties my feet wide to the tires of the bike. He takes duct tape and places it over my shield. I am now gagged and blinded. Then it strikes my bare ass. Master is using his belt to warm my ass. I hear my moaning and heavy breathing in the helmet, at times stopping to hear the whoosh and smack to my skin. Master starts with easy, but increases in tempo and strength. Then he starts into my mind with verbal explanations as to why I am being treated so. I feel my dick grow, as I picture Master in his full leathers, helmet and boots, beating my naked ass, as I am covered in leather and bound to his bike. The warmth of the well used engine near my dick as it grows. Each blow makes me feel the plug in my ass, the plug that has been there for hours! The pain in my ass and on it begins to get intense and I struggle in the bondage. I sweat even more than before and feel it dripping from my forehead. Then there is one major strike and all is quiet. I listen to my breathing for a moment. And realize that Master has left me.

As my ass burns, I want to reach my dick and stroke off! I am his slave secured to his motorcycle. Then I feel action on my wrists and Master is releasing me. He also releases my feet. He moves around to sit on the bike. I am in his position when we ride. I feel his warmth still there, the gas tank pressing against my naked dick and balls. He lays me back and my head falls off the back end of the bike. He secures my feet down to the front wheel then my arms down my side and to bars on the bike. I feel his gloved hand take a hold of my dick. It is hard and standing straight up. He starts to describe how he likes the way he sees me and perhaps some of his riding buddies should come over later when I'm tied in the prior position and fuck me. He works my dick over and over with his dry glove, at times, my pre-cum lubes it. I moan in my helmet, I want to release me load, but Master is toying with me. I struggle on the bike, trying to move my hands to my dick, but I can't.

I sweat in my leather more, some of the leather has been on me over 24 hours now. Master reaches in my jacket and pinches my tits, as I scream, he strokes so fast that I know I must shoot. And as he pinches again, I feel the tank of this machine pressing my balls and ass. I am secured to a powerful thing, as a powerful Man controls me, making me struggle before him. I shoot my load, and Master continues to work my dick as I drain my balls. I struggle for now things are more sensitive. He laughs, and then releases me, returning me to the prior position secured to the bike.

I feel the plug removed and then my Masters dick entering me. I want him so deep in me, he pulls in and out, making me feel his power now. His hand pulls on my shoulder, as I slam into his bike with his force in my ass. He slams hard and harder, enjoying my ass, for it is his to enjoy. I feel his leather on my hairless skin, breathing hard in my helmet. He takes his time, as he finally shoots, in what has to be hours after he first entered. Slowly, he removes himself and releases me.

He grabs my dick and leads me to the bed room. He pushes me on the bed, removes my helmet and gag. He lies beside me, both of us in our leather, me still hooded. He starts stroking me, as I do him. We look into each others eyes, knowing what we need and deep kiss each other in the fire filled passion that we have for each other. Holding each other in our leather covered bodies.

Final Tears

This was the night, finally after months of being apart, Master and I were going to be together again. There was so much to catch up on during our time together. We had five days to be with one another, to once again hold each other and remember our special feelings. My flight had arrived early, so I waited at the gate for Sir to arrive. I was dressed just as he required me to be, with my bleachers snug fit reminding me of Sir. Black boots, red shirt and bomber jacket completed the required look. Under I wore no underwear, and none was packed, since Sir requires that I be naked under my clothing for him. I had shaved my hair before leaving home, so it was nice and smooth for him.

Out of the corner of my eye I caught movement towards me. The gate area was totally empty and was far from crowds. When I turned my head, I saw Master briefly, as his black leather gloved hand reached for my mouth and gagged me tight. He stood before me, squeezing, as I took in my Master. He was wearing his black boots, camos, collared polo shirt and flight jacket. He had shaved his head; he was my skinhead Master tonight. His other gloved hand reached for my crotch, he smiled as he felt me getting hard in my tight jeans. "Welcome, boi," he said. His hand left my mouth, to be replaced by his lips and his tongue filling my mouth. His gloved hand grabbed the back of my head and pulled me into him. I reached around and grabbed his ass and pulled him towards me. My only thoughts were of how glad I was finally feeling my Master again.

He pulled away, smiled at me, spitting in my face. He asked if I had my chain collar, I took it out of my backpack and Sir locked it around my neck again. He removed my dog tags that I normally wear when not wearing my collar and put them in his pocket. I was home. He stuffed the collar down my shirt, the cold metal on my skin made me shiver a bit. He grabbed my neck and pulled me forward and up and we headed down the concourse. I stayed one pace behind Master, keeping in step with him. His head was high, he was confident and he was beautiful in my eyes. I felt confident also, as we passed through the security point on the way to the baggage claim. The area was empty, as I picked up my bag and we head to Sir's truck.

He had parked away from the terminal in a dark corner and the walk was a long one. I put my bag in the bed of the truck and Sir ordered me around to his door. I quickly arrived before him. He pointed down and I knew he wanted me to kneel. I dropped down, with my head bowed.

"Kiss the boots, boi." was all he said as I went down and kissed them. I had learned from Sir earlier never to go beyond the command. If he wanted them licked, he would've told me. He did not. Sir opened his button fly on his camo pants to reveal a well worn dirty jock. Behind it, he revealed his cock. His gloved hands came around the back of my head, drawing me near his dick. I opened my mouth and took it in. He was not fully hard as he wanted me to just let it lay. Then the warm salty taste of piss filled my throat and I once again gave full service to my Master. He stroked my head as I kept up with the flow, which wasn't easy. I know it was hard for him to keep from stopping as my warm mouth pleased his cock. He pulled out and started pissing on my head, as it ran down my face and neck, soaking into the collar of my shirt. Once done, he pointed at his cock again and I cleaned it with my tongue. He put it back behind the leather jock and buttoned up his camos.

Master asked for my rubber hood and I told him it was in my backpack. He reached in the truck bed and rummaged through my bags. He found it and slipped it over my head, made easier by the piss. The hood has only eye and nose holes. He lifted me up and told me to get in the truck. Once in, we both were seat belted and Sir pulled my rubber head to his crotch. There I would lie as he went through the toll booth and out to the freeway. As he drove, he was stroking my rubber pissed covered head with his leather glove, holding it over my nose for long stretches of time to let me take in the warm leather smell. At times, he would tighten the hold and I couldn't breath. I was able to stroke his legs, keeping my hands down, as he ordered. I don't think many could see me in Sir's lap, perhaps a free show for the truckers. But at that moment, I was glad to be with Sir again. I was back in the arms of the Man I love.

That night we fell in love all over again. There was talking, lots of it. But there was more touching, kissing, hugging. I was able to taste his cock in my mouth over and over. It was sweet, strong and filled my mouth, letting me know who I am, my Master's slave. We wrestled, laughed and enjoyed the site of each other in our eyes, so close. We fell asleep just before sunrise, with Sir holding me, his cock planted in his slave's ass.

I woke startled and disoriented. I was gagged with duct tape, with Master slamming my ass with his dick. My hands had been bound above my head and my feet spread eagled. Master was enjoying me helpless before him as he stated he loved waking and fucking his slave's ass. He'd reach under me, grabbing my dick with his gloved hand. He started stroking, as it grew in his fingers. I would hear Sir comment on me being his, owned and forever fucked by him in the future. And he would even control me shooting my load, so that we did it at the same time. Harder and harder he would work, slamming deeper into me. He would pass beyond our prior session and make me feel him whole. He would slap my ass, I'm sure it was getting red. He was dominating me, controlling me as I was getting closer. Through my breathing and moaning he sensed it, and he was getting close also. He reminded me of his huge cock filling his slave's ass, I was taking it because that was my role in life. To please him, and I was pleasing him fully this morning.

"This is just the beginning, boi, just the beginning. You're mine, I own you," he screamed as he was shooting his load in his slave's ass. My body tensed and I shot my load into the sheets of the bed. Master stroked, stroked and stroked, bringing out every last drop. It had been so long for the both of us. He pulled his gloved hand from beneath me, wiping cum on my face and over the gag. He laid on me, stroking my head.

"I love you boi." I could only moan I loved him in return.

By 2 in the afternoon, we were showered and heading out the door. We were going to visit an amusement park and dinner after. It was a warm day, but I was dressed as Sir wanted me. I was in my camos, boots, black shirt. He was wearing jeans, his 14 hole boots and white shirt with Yamaha logo on it. The day was spent being friends, enjoying life and laughing and getting to know each other more. I know I had a good time and Master told me he did also, on our way home.

It was late by the time we arrived home, so we check out email and spent quiet time on the sofa. Then it was off to bed, since we were both very tired. The next two days were filled with normal days, nothing intense in the BDSM front. I remembered my love and devotion to Master every minute. Never did it leave me. He worked with me again on learning more commands in military regiment, as he wanted a military order to his household and his slave was going to follow every command. Everyday it was a test to remember and learn more. We also worked on PT requirements, with Sir working along with me. At times we wrestled and teased each other; other times it was just sitting in front of the computer watching Sir conquer his video game. One night we visited the bar, for Sir really wanted to show me off. It was a simple night, more relaxed than our last time in a bar. I enjoyed meeting Sir's friends and hoped that I made Sir proud by showing them respect. At night we would sleep quietly. Sometimes Sir would wake me and I would take his piss so he wouldn't have to leave bed. And of course, I was able to relax Sir with my talent at massage. I so enjoy those moments together. There is nothing more than me touching him, relaxing him, and he loving his boi for showing him care.

Two days before my departure, things seemed to change. Sure I had screwed up a few times during our time together and had my ass beat by the SAP gloves, but it was nothing major. But this day, I ended up hog tied, in my full BDU's and boots for not following a movement command. Sir was pissed at me. He kicked me a few time and the bondage was tight. I was gagged with a pair of his dirty underwear, and watched his boots as he paced before me wondering if I could ever be trained properly. I had never seen him so upset, and I was getting more upset for I really felt I had failed him. I was out the door as soon as he released me, I just knew it.

His boot lifted my chin to see him in my eyes. A large load of snot fell to my face, "boi, I didn't want it to come to this, but it has to." With that he kicks my head up and removes his boot. I hit the floor hard with my chin, jarring myself. I hear him rummaging though some drawers behind me. Then I feel it behind my neck, cold, steel. It is his gun, I know it. But I'm not worried, he had shown it to me last time and it was a prop gun, no barrel.

"Forget what you know slave, times have changed," around he pulls his silver plated hand gun. This was not the gun Sir had before. As he holds it between my eyes he explains that this one is not a fake. He drops out the cartridge that holds the ammunition and it is loaded. And I see that the barrel is open. He slams the cartridge back in and points it flush with my forehead, "You've fucked up, haven't you?"

I didn't know what to do; this was not as settling as I had been with Sir. I nodded my head yes to please him. He shoved me across the floor with his boot. He swore and talked to me like true scum. I was feeling it also, I wanted loose to show him I was sorry. I don't know how, but I didn't want him angry with me!

"I had such hopes...now wasted," he walks behind him and puts his motorcycle helmet on my head, which he has taped up the shield. I think I hear him leave the room.

I am left for what seems like hours in the hog tie. The pressure on my chest is strong, the stiffness in my limbs hard, this is not pleasure. Over and over I go through my mind as to what I have done to bring Master and myself to this point. It is warm in the helmet and I feel sweat dropping across my face. This is the helmet that Sir wears while riding on his motorcycle. Motorcycling with Sir was one of our dreams. Now it seems that dream wasn't going to be coming true.

Something knocks my head hard and I am aware that Sir must have returned. He begins to undo the hog tie and my arms and legs fall with relief. I'm kicked and ordered to stand. I do so as quickly as possible. The helmet is removed and Sir is in his BDU's. I notice his arm with his Staff Sgt. rank. He orders me to attention, I snap to.

"Forward march."

I follow his commands as I step off, and we head out the door. It is night, dark and a cool breeze breaking the late summer heat. Sir has parked his truck in the garage and we enter. In the back is his cage. I am ordered to halt and attention. Sir comes to me, taking the leather hood and slides it on my head. The gag is tightly strapped, and the eyes closed from sight. I am lead up to the bed of the truck and to the cage. He secures my feet before me, as I have to bend over to fit in. A dowel of wood goes between my legs, my arms brought under it. My hands are gloved then secured under the doweling and before my ankles. Rope is further secured to my neck, bringing me forward. Sir unbuttons my shirt and puts on tit clamps. I am pushed into the cage and it is locked shut. A tarp is dropped over and tied down. I can smell the plastic and it begins to get warm. I hear Sir getting in the truck and starting it. The movement rocks me and makes me realize how helpless I am. As he increases speed, the noise of the tarp flapping in the wind is deafening. I sometimes slam into the sides of the cage as I know Sir is taking the corners fast on purpose. The tit clamps dig in on each pot hole, but eventually my tits go numb.

Over time the road gets rougher and rougher, the speeds less. I have no idea as to where I am being taken, for I barely know the area. And following turns and such would do me no good. Then the truck stops and the engine turned off.

Silence was all I heard as I was removed from the cage, strung up between two trees out in the middle of nowhere in California. The moon was the only light, the warmth rising from the grass and dirt. As I was released, Sir wasn't gentle with me. He would strike me hard, kick me and even piss on me. He was oblivious to me, I was now nothing to him but a puppet to entertain his sadistic ideas. He had removed the eye flap on the hood but the rest remained. My shirt had been removed, the rope dug into my wrists and ankles of my boots. I had been like this for a short while. The whoosh was my only warning as the flogger struck my bare back. It was hard and it stung. I was moved forward with the blast, and upon returning back, was hit with another. He was not being gentle as before to start. It was strong and he was fucking beating me like he most likely had wanted to all along. He was showing me who was the Master, and who was the helpless slave.

I couldn't escape and eventually took the only way to relieve the pain, yelling into the gag. Master laughed and said I "could yell all I wanted, no one would hear." He struck me even harder. The flogging would continue. Then he would come before me, smiling and shaking his head. "It is really too bad."

I looked at him with a questioning look.

"You don't get it do you, asshole. It's over. I'm done with you. You're not serious, you screw up, your lazy and you're a fuck head," with that he flogged my chest. The pain was getting intense and I was trying to hold back the tears. I had never been taken this far in pain. I believed that he was going to abuse me to the max and send me home. How could I have screwed up so bad, disappointed him so. I love him, he said he loved me, but we were Master and slave and that was very important to us both. The flogging continued as the tears began to fill my eyes.

"Fuck, you're crying, you fucking piss ant!"

He slammed me harder, striking the tit clamps and I screamed into the gag as they fell off. He moved next to me and shoved his gloved thumb into my tit. I squirmed in my bondage, yelling in pain, tears coming down my cheeks under the leather of the hood. I was yelling for him to stop, to let me go. Though the gag it didn't sound like much. But deep inside I didn't want to go, not to leave. Just make the pain stop, let me know that he did love me. This wasn't a show now, he was pissed and I was learning who my Master truly was.

He stood back, his eyes looked deeper and more evil and powerful than I had ever seen. He was enjoying himself; he was enjoying his power over me. At least I could sense that I was pleasing him, but for the last time. Never had anyone taken me to this place in my mind, brought me to tears. But I wanted to be strong for him also, the tears came, I couldn't help it.

Eventually, he tired of toying with me and let me loose. But I was not allowed long to be free. I was lead to a fence and sat down. He tied me to it tightly with rope, including my head secured forward and up. If I lowered it, I would choke. As he reached to his side, I then noticed his holster. He pulled out his silver weapon and asked if I remember it. I shook my head yes, as best as I could.

He started to walk backwards, never taking his eyes off me, smiling and kissing the gun. He lifted the gun into the air and pointed it towards the stars. I jumped when I heard the shot. Fuck, this was a real gun. He looked at me and nodded slightly as to say, yes boi, it's real.

He lowered the gun towards me. I closed my eyes. Master yelled at me to keep them open. I couldn't believe this; I was struggling to get free. He yelled again for me to sit still. He fired a shot and it went by me, I heard a can fall.

"This is gun play, slave!" and he laughed.

He fired off several shots. They seemed to get closer, I wanted out of there. I wanted to stop him, I wanted to cry. I was loosing my Man, Master the one I loved with all my heart!

When he was done, he came to me and dropped the empty chamber in my lap. He pulled two more out of his coat pocket, letting me know that was all he had. Fuck, that was way too much and he was getting too close. He moved closer, pushing my sore bruised back against the rough wall. "Who's Master?" he laughs.

He returned to his position and began firing again. He didn't take his time, his shot is good. Being a former Marine, I have no doubt that he could shoot me when he was ready. And I believe that it was going to come. I wasn't hard, I was fucking scared. I would run away the minute I could. I would get away from this man. Emotionally I was a wreck in my heart. I had been so devoted to him.

When he was done, he dropped the second cartridge in my lap. He removed my bounds and stood me up, the cartridges falling to the ground.

He tied me at the end of the truck bed, with the tail gate down. My hands were above my head, stretched, my legs pulled up and back, as I laid on my back. He worked my BDU pants down exposing my ass. He was rough, violent and quick in his actions. Getting them down he stands before me, "The final scene, boi."

He reaches in his pocket and grabs the last cartridge, snapping it in. He takes the gun and slides around my bare ass. It is cool and my skin reacts as I struggle in my helpless position. He works the barrel to my hole and in it. He begins fucking my ass with a loaded gun, as he reminds me over and over verbally. He squeezes my balls tightly, ordering me to get fucking hard. "Take this like a man!" In and out it goes, over and over. The steel warms as my ass takes it in time and time again.

He stops, pulling it out. He works the gag off my head and stuffs my mouth with my ass covered gun. He orders me to clean it, as I do with my tongue.

"The gun is loaded slave, loaded and in your mouth. Clean it or I will pull the trigger." I can barely see his leathered finger pulling back on the trigger. Emotionally this is getting to me again. I am getting stiff and sore in my position, my evil Master has a loaded weapon in my mouth, as I taste my ass on my tongue. His other gloved hand is working my cock, and I am trying to get hard. But

I am not going for this. This is too much.

He lets go of the gun and tells me to keep it in my mouth. I do so.

"It's time slave, it's time for you to go all the way. To where only a few go." with that he drops his BDU's and his hard cock stands straight out. He grabs his gun, and immediate slams his cock in my ass. It hurts like hell as I scream around the gun. He has never fucked me this hard, never. This is rape, violent evil rape. He is showing me his true power over his slave's ass. I am his slave, for the collar is still around my neck. He is smiling evilly as he fucks me.

"I want you to watch me screw your pitiful ass, slave! Watch the Master you could've served power you!" his crotch slams into me. His head goes back, the gun moving up and down in my mouth, at times knocking my teeth. He strokes my dick over and over, I am getting hard. Then he stops, "You're on your own now." and he laughs.

Then I notice the chain around my neck tightening, I look and find his free hand holding a rope that has to be tied to the back of my collar. He yells at me, verbally abuses me, how things are over, I have screwed up so much, I am a loser and that he is going to take me out for no one deserves to deal with me. He is going to ride me to the end. I wanted military power, I have it. I wanted to dominated, I am until the end.

All this was running in my head, this was beyond any fantasy I had ever had, it was too real. He showed me the safety; it wasn't on and shoved the gun further in my throat. I choked on it once as my breathing got more difficult as the chain pulled tighter. And his fucking never stopped, it was hard and brutal. I broke, the tears were flowing, I wanted to go. I started begging to be set free. I was sorry and would leave. He would only laugh, saying it wasn't an option, I had accepted his collar.

With pure frustration I struggled in the bondage, he only fucked me harder and his eyes showed he was so turned on by this. He fucked and I wondered how he could be holding out. Then he stopped, sweat pouring off his head. Staying inside me, he reached into a pocket and pulled out the keys to the collar lock. He unlocked it and removed it, tossing it in the air, landing in the distance.

"Don't want no one knowing I owned you," as my tears calmed a bit. Then the realization that it was over hit me. He had removed the collar. I broke down, screaming no. He slammed me harder and fucked me like a machine. I bawled like a baby and he was fucking me more. It was as if that was what he wanted. He wanted me to break down.

"Time's up fuck head."

He fucked harder and quicker, pulling back the trigger. My breathing was intense, between the tears and sweat. I can't believe I was going to die. He smiled at me, verbally taunting me as it pulled the trigger back and back. I looked at those eyes, the ones I loved so deeply, trying to see some hope of redemption in there. The sweat dropped from his forehead as he smiled and bore into me with those eyes. He was reaching climax, as he started stroking my dick. I was getting hard; I couldn't believe it through all this!

He shot his load and I heard the gun click, yelling!

The gun came out of my mouth immediately, Master smiled as he shot his last load, I was shooting also. I wasn't dead, the gun was not loaded, and I broke down crying. He looked at me, his sweat covered face and a slight movement to his crotch.

"I love you boi." he whispered. "I truly love you and need you."

I cried even harder, wanting to reach him and hold him. I can't tell for sure, but there might have been tears mixed in his sweat also. He laid upon my chest hugging me, pulling out his cock. I felt his cum drip out and down my ass. Slowly he helped me calm down emotionally. I know that Sir had wanted to break me emotionally since our first time, so seem me go beyond my limits and do it with him. He took me so deep, but at the same time, made it impossible for me to ever love another Man. He was so happy and tender in the moments after. He kissed my lips, my head, and my dick. He loved me.

Whispering to me, "It's time for you to be here with me, 24/7. I want you here. Tomorrow we'll start plans for you to move." He pauses and kisses me with passion and strength and I return it. When he is done, I look at him. "I love you." I smile, "Master".

Boi Made Master

Deep in my heart I knew it could happen, but when it did I lost my breath for a moment. Across the room he entered, in his skin kit. He always took pride in his camo pants, Fred Perry shirt with braces and his 20 hole boots. I remember the day I gave him those boots and how much he was surprised. I remember the look in his eyes and the smile on his face as he put it on. Everything had to fit just right and it did on him. It was a year ago that I presented him with those boots and now he was wearing them without me around.

Part of me expected him to be with his new boi, but he was alone. Heads turned as he wandered the aisles of the leather gathering. I don't know if he saw me or not. If he didn't, I'm sure he and everyone else heard my heart beating. My buddy asked me a question and I was snapped back to the reality around me. He was purchasing a leather jacket and wanted to know how it looked on him. I smiled, letting him know that it fit very well and that it was a good price. He modeled in the mirror a bit more and I put the boots and the Man in them out of my mind.

At dinner that night, I told my bud that I had seen the Man that had me collared last year at the event. He was a good friend asking me if I was alright and how I was feeling. He knew the hurt I felt when I found out the lies and cheating. For so many months we both talked of trust and dedication, but it was a one way street. Two days after finding out, while talking with my bud on the phone I broke down in a crying and emotional release, the likes I had never experienced. That is when you feel so alone, when your friend is on the other end of a telephone, no one to hold you any longer, only a voice saying that things will be ok.

After dinner we headed to the main bar for the night. It was packed to the rafters with men in leather, uniforms and boots. A boi's dream to say the least. While I was never a bar hound, I had been visiting them on occasion and found them more successful than in the past. This night was no different. A very handsome and well built Man came up to me to let me know his boots were scuffed and dusty. I didn't need anymore invitation. Through the leather clad legs, I made my way down and started licking his boots. He puffed on his cigar as he lifted his boot up to make sure that my mouth and tongue were filled with his leather Wesco Engineers. Once or twice my ass was swatted by someone walking by. But this Boot Master let me know that I was doing a good job and to continue. My tongue worked the leather like it was an ice cream cone, swirling the leather, my saliva deep into the hide, down along the crevasse of the sole to the leather, then up the tall shafts that his leather pants were tucked into. On occasion he would reach down and pat my shaved head with his Damascus gloved hand, with a "Good boi," for reassurance.

As I completed the second boot, he reached down and quickly snapped a pair of handcuffs on my wrists behind my back. He raised me to my feet and planted a deep long kiss. His cigar filled my taste buds as his tongue ravished my mouth. His leather gloved hand pulled me away as I started to move my tongue towards his lips. He turned me around and started marching me towards the exit. In the cab, he continued to rape my mouth with his tongue, the sound of our leather intermixing with each other and against the vinyl seat. Though the drive to the hotel not a word was spoken for our lips never parted.

As I laid in bed, the pink of the sunrise was filling the curtains. I looked over at the naked Man that I was next too, his legs over mine. He would have made others jealous of his build. A sharp cut of hair on his head that was crisp and short. He had a distinctive ink on his back. He looked as if he worked out on a regular basis. I could hear my bud telling me the next time I saw him that I went home with the prize of the night. It was something my ego needed these days.

I don't remember what happened after returning to his room but I know we both experienced some mind numbing play. He was totally in control the entire time. His bondage was flawless, though I didn't see much of it. He worked his way into my head verbally, bringing me to climax once, or maybe it was twice. I know I felt his warm man juice over my chest and back a few times.

After he woke, we spent several hours just lying naked, next to each other. We talked about where we've been, where we'd like to go. But I knew inside that he was not going to be my life Master. We had fun last night, plain and simple. That is what happens at these events most of the time, a weekend of sex and fun, then back to the depressing world of trying to find the guy that will be a lifetime. We kissed and I returned to my room for a shower and another nap before heading out for some food.

I was just about finished with putting on my motorcycle leathers and MX boots, when there was a knock on the door. I snapped down the final latch on my boots and got up to answer it. When I opened, it was him. He was in his bleachers, boots, leather cop gloves and black bomber jacket. He pushed me into my room with a force that I didn't expect and shut the door behind him. I stumbled towards the bed.

He was pissed as he moved towards me and started yelling. I figured this might happen if he had a chance to get me alone. He didn't like the way that I was going after him after he had cheated me out of some promises he made. He was young and thought he could get away with it. I was older and knew better. It certainly wasn't the way I wanted the relationship to end, of course, I didn't want him to be living with someone else and lying about it either. But that is the way things go sometimes. Sure I was his boi, but when he admitted his dishonesty that collar came off and I became a man again. And I wasn't going to be taken by some young punk like him.

He made a move to try to strike me and I ducked. I had weight on my side and I shoved him to the bed. We wrestled on the bed, his face turning red as a hanky in the back pocket of a fister. He wouldn't shut up and he went on and on about how he was going to show me! As we wrestled I finally got him on his back, his legs were trying to kick me in my back, but he couldn't bend them far enough. I grabbed the handcuffs that were lying on the table by the bed and after a long struggle got them on him. He was really pissed now, but I remembered something about the times we had that he seemed to forget. While holding his legs, I dug through my bag and found a roll of duct tape that I hoped someone would use on me during the weekend. Tightly I wrapped it around his ankles and over the boots and denim. Then I did the same around his knees.

He was raving about how I was going to get my ass fucked big time for doing this to him. I chuckled, him saying that to me, as he was now squirming on my bed, helpless and in bondage. I was getting tired of the random threats so I grabbed a sock that I had worn yesterday and shoved it in his mouth. I wrapped the tape around his face and neck so tight; I thought I was going to pop his head off.

I tossed the tape to the floor, turned him on his back and straddled him. I looked into those eyes of his that I had fallen in love with, "Seem to me we've been here before." He was quiet now, realizing that he didn't have much choice and that yes he had been tied up by me before. There was one thing that no one knew about the year that I was his boi and he was my Master; that the only bondage in the relationship was when I tied him up and played with him. This Master that turned everyone's head, that made everyone so hot and bothered was only a Master because I let everyone believe he was. I stared right at him and reminded him of how I was in control of so many of the events. And how he was such a chicken shit in the end that he couldn't even end the relationship, he had to lie about it. He had to enter into a relationship with a boi that would go beyond the trust and respect of a Master/slave relationship that was very public and help the Master hide it. A Master that let me dress him the way I felt he should be dressed, not as he saw himself. But mostly because he did know who he was. He was trying to be something he was not. I was a boi that believed more in the Master than the Master believed in himself.

Calmly I brought back many events to this helpless Master. Oh sure, I realized that I was to blame for things progressing as they did, the promises and talk week after week and the events that never did happen. How many other boi's did he play with that I didn't know about? While the entire time, I devoted myself to him for the entire year. No play with anyone that entire time. For no one could do me the way he did. The few times we actually had sex, I had to instigate it. And how foolish I was to not see how he took pains to keep the relationship hidden, for he was always hoping for something better to come along. And along it came in a boi that wouldn't respect the relationship. Of course, I will never know what part this Master had in this, or what lies he was telling that boi. And in the end this Master couldn't keep his promises of completing his commitments.

I couldn't believe myself when I spit in his face. Through the entire time since the trust was broken, I had taken the high road. Only my close friends knew the real reason why things had ended. And when others spoke poorly of him I stopped them. After all, I did love the Man and there were wonderful, though short, times. This Master was the one that had turned ugly and didn't respect me in the end. The one that showed him the most respect he may have ever had was the one he shit on the most.

I looked at him and told him that he really is a boi inside; he could never be a Master, for he didn't know what it meant. I had tried to show him and build that in him, with him. But in the end he couldn't realize it. I slapped his face. Damn, it felt good. I slapped it again, harder. He yelled in the gag. He tried to buck me off, but I hit him again. Something was coming up inside me, something that I had never felt. I ripped off his gag and rolled him to the floor. I stuck my boot in his face and yelled at him to start licking. He refused. I kicked him with the other boot and you know slowly, he started to put his tongue out and licked it. I took my other boot and dug it into his crotch.

"You are licking your boi's boots, Sir." I said snidely.

I expected a 'fuck you' out of him, I didn't get it. He was licking the boot fairly well. I reached down to his crotch with my gloved hand and I closed my eyes when I felt his hard dick. This Master was enjoying his position. In reality, he wasn't a Master.

I put my other boot in his face and he worked on that. I decided to let him realize his situation on his own in silence. I sort of wished I had some other gear with me, I would've been a better top. But I wasn't a top; I never had it in me. And frankly, I was not hard in the least in doing this. But my mind was getting into this. For once again, I was showing this man who he is. I had tried to show him what a Master would be like. He obviously couldn't handle it, cause he failed at the basics.

I pulled him off the floor and put his stomach on the bed. I was not myself in these moments. I went in the bathroom, closed the door and pissed on the sock that had been in his mouth. I returned and shoved it in without compassion. This was about brutality now, something I had only dreamed of happening to me. I taped the sock back in. Then I rolled him on his back and undid his belt, pulled down the zipper. He was struggling a little bit, but not as much as a Master would when he was about to be fucked by his ex-boi.

I pulled down his pants and leather jock as much as I could. I found something sharp and cut the tape on his knees and ankles. The little bit of rope I did have went around each ankle and I was able to spread them wide and rope them over his head to the headboard. I wanted this, inside it was telling me this. But I wasn't hard enough. I dug through my bag of goodies and found my leather hood. He knew about this hood, for together we had it custom designed for me. Months later during a trouble spot I sent it to him showing my commitment and he responded on how much the hood had meant to me and that he almost cried. Yet, he had no qualms of putting the hood on the boi he was lying to me about. That special hood that was designed for me was on the cheater boi.

I laced it up and I got harder, for I could smell the leather in my nose. I stroked my dick with my leather gloved hand, and it grew. I thought about the time that he fucked me for the first time, last year after we had shared some of the deepest moments of our lives. He had rolled me over, as I was naked and with lube inserted his dick deep into my ass. It was powerful, brutal and I was yelling into the bed. He called me every name a boi should be called as the Man I loved, as my Master fucked me and until he shot his load in me. It was a moment I had never felt and one that I have never experienced since.

In my hand my dick had grown to full size and a sliver of liquid was now dripping from it. I knew that the cuffs must be digging into his wrists by now, but I didn't fucking care. I wasn't myself, as I looked in his eyes. He was fearful in some sense, angry in another.

"Your boi is going to fuck his Master."

Through his gag came a loud yell, which I am sure was "fuck you." But it was half hearted for inside he knew he wanted this. It was who he really was. Something took hold of me, something I never felt. I entered his ass with force; I threw my head back and took in the smell of leather around my head. I had never fucked anyone in my life and now I was fucking the Man that I had loved more than anyone else in my life. It was slow to start; I didn't know what I was doing. But my body knew exactly what to do. My hips started thrusting and he was moaning and yelling in his pissed soaked gag. I lowered my head to look in his eyes again. His anger was turning to submission. He was learning that he was conquered. And I knew that he was only because he let himself.

As I fucked him I remembered the times lying next to him, massaging his back, the kisses that would melt my heart and the surprise of him holding my hand in the park. Where did that come from and where did it go.

I was reaching a point of climax and emotions started to take over. I could feel things moving in me that I seldom felt. My dick exploded in this man's ass and I collapsed on his chest crying with so much anger and relief. All I could get out of my mouth was a weak, "I loved you."

And the emotions continued. I pulled out and slowly looked up at him. That is when I saw it, a tear streaming from his eye.

Maybe, just maybe, he still had something left inside for me. Perhaps I was wrong to do what I did. I cleaned myself up as I left him laying there. I stopped myself and told me that I was not to blame what had happen here. I was used more than I could have known. I refused to not trust others because of him.

I pulled my leathers up and took off the hood. I tossed it in the bag and cleaned up a bit.

I looked at him, "You know, I think I've always known you better than you thought."

He started crying into the gag, I had hit the nail on the head. I went to him and held his head to me. I kissed him on his gag and looked in his eyes. Yup it was still there, we both cared about each other. But today was not the start of things over again. No, I'm not sure if it would ever happen, but I know inside that there is that small part that would listen to him if he called and wanted to discuss it.

I kissed him again and stood. I went to the room door and opened it. I found a pen and wrote a little sign and laid it below his asshole. I went to the door and looked back at him.

"boi, this boi is going to find you some real Masters," with that I headed down the hall.

About the Author

Taking his first step into leather and bondage over ten years ago, ty dehner found that memories were not enough and began writing about his adventures. Several of these true life experiences were published in Bound & Gagged magazine. As his experiences grew, so did his ideas and he started to write fiction. His first published work was "Skin boi". It was well received on the internet and to this day is one of his most requested pieces.

With the explosion of the internet there were many new places to share bondage fiction. But ty found that many of the sites didn't last and he felt there was room for something better for all of us that were into man to man bondage and gear action. In 1999, he created the online magazine Ropedweb. Over time, he published his own stories, along with fetish pictures and videos that he also wrote and directed. By the time Ropedweb came to an end in 2005 it had been viewed in 160 countries around the world.

Since his introduction as a submissive into the leather BDSM world, ty has been involved with many community activities including sponsoring the International Deaf Leather contest in Seattle, taking over the historic New World Rubbermen and donating the contents to the Leather Archives in Chicago, marching in the pride parade in Vancouver, B.C., creating exciting web sites for Dungeon on the Bay, the Jail Training Center, Matt Lyons, and Ironstar Media. ty dehner has attended many fetish events including International Mr. Leather in Chicago, Rubbout in Vancouver, B.C., Dore Alley Street Fair in San Francisco and has enjoyed meeting the many leather, rubber, sport gear fans that attend.

Through all his writing he has had one focus, to share his experiences and dreams with others in the hopes that they will step out into this exciting and creative community to become a part of it. He has always enjoyed hearing from those that enjoy his work, as well as those that share their experiences after reading his work. If that includes you, you can contact ty via his web site: www.tydehner.com

ty dehner continues to write while locked in his hood and leather, serving his Master on an island off the shores of Washington.

www.ingramcontent.com/pod-product-compliance
Lightning Source LLC
Chambersburg PA
CBHW071225260626
47162CB00004B/1427

* 9 7 8 1 9 3 4 6 2 5 2 6 2 *